AN APPARENT HORIZON

RICARDO WILSON

Printed in the United States of America

First Edition
1 2 3 4 5 6 7 8 9

Cover: Dionne Lee. *Challenger Deep*, 2019. Image courtesy of the artist.
Interior and cover design by PANK

ISBN 978-1-948587-20-4

PANK Magazine
PANK Books

To purchase multiple copies or book events, readings and author signings contact books@pankmagazine.com

AN APPARENT HORIZON

& OTHER STORIES

BY RICARDO WILSON

for

Meredith and Tanner

Contents

threshold

They told themselves they were not running. They were traveling North for good, listening to the nun sing Climb Ev'ry Mountain. It was the only thing the son would sleep to, though even he was awake. The mother played Black People like she'd played License Plates in a Volkswagen bus as a kid. Though it was not quite Canada, the father thought of Ishmael's Dream.

A mooring post, a cross placed in the thicket of a new shore, a gallows. Crossing a threshold meant something, even if that meaning would unreal. And even if they would not feel the unrealing.

Saturday

Today, Saturday, Carol and Aisha will drive to Irvine and collect Donnie's cremated remains. It is early morning. Carol knocks on her daughter's door to wake her but she is already up and dressed, hooded in her brother's cardinal-red sweatshirt despite the building heat and wearing her home-cut jean shorts and flip-flops. She is listening to her iPod and sitting with legs splayed on the carpet, gluing fake jewels on her freshly painted toes. During the school year Aisha is not allowed to paint her nails. It's how Carol, the youngest in a family of girls, was raised. But with just a week left before summer break the assistant principal had called to let Carol know that Aisha would be passed to the next grade.

Standing at the door, Carol notes that she and her daughter do not share body types. Or that they are beginning to differentiate in this way. Though exaggerated because Aisha's legs are pressed against the carpet, Aisha is much heavier in the thighs, even at fourteen. Carol knocks again on the door and Aisha looks up from her nails and holds up two fingers to suggest a time for her mother to wait.

It is the first time they have been in the car, or out of the apartment, since Tuesday. Since Carol's son had killed a neighborhood boy in what most of the local press is calling an accident and then hung himself in her garage. On Wednesday, Aisha had had the company of her best friend Caitlyn until the girls were delivered a cum-spattered pizza. Caitlyn's brother, home from college, was sent to collect her.

Carol's older-model silver Honda Civic is parked at the mouth of the driveway, away from the garage, and is thickly covered in the purple stain of the flowers from the overhanging jacaranda. There are no news trucks waiting at the curb blocking the driveway as there had been on the previous days. Yesterday there had been only one, Local Channel 49. Carol had watched on and off for six hours through the blinds of the front window as an anchorwoman in the back of the truck continually primped in a handheld mirror waiting for someone to come out of the upper unit of the duplex on 78th Street in Westchester, the only rental on the street. She interviewed neighbors as they came home from work, interviewed their children. Almost all pointed to Carol's garage and then to Carol's front door. The anchorwoman came up the steps and knocked on two occasions.

They arrive at the Patel and Sons mortuary and Carol instructs her daughter to stay in the car. The sun is high and the car will soon start to bake but Carol does not suggest her daughter open a window. When her mother is a few steps away, Aisha leans across the driver's seat to tap her knuckles on the window. Carol turns and Aisha makes a gesture for the keys.

She takes the headphones out of her ears and turns the radio to a pop station, removes her hood and rests her tightly braided head on the glass and stares in the direction of the sign above the one-story, dark-brown building.

Inside the mortuary, Carol walks all the way to the counter before an Indian man wearing a tightfitting short-sleeved shirt with gold embroidery removes his reading glasses and looks up from his papers.

"How may I help you?"

She gives her name, but it does not register an immediate response.

"Donald Crawford is my son," she says. "We spoke on the phone."

"Yes."

He rings a call bell that is fastened to the counter.

He taps his pen as he waits for someone to emerge from the back office. Carol can see a head moving beyond the saloon-style doors. She looks back to the man with papers spread before him, his thin black chest hairs escaping a shirt that has been poorly laundered—strings hang from the embroidery and there is a pinkish stain below his collar. He turns to look in the back office, rings the bell again and mutters an apology to Carol, who stands straight and has pulled her lips tight.

"How did you find us?" he says finally.

Carol wonders if it has been a topic of discussion among the employees this morning.

"My daughter found you on the computer."

He smiles and presses his palms to the counter. "It is my daughter who has designed our website."

Carol pulls in her lips again. "Is this going to take long?"

"It will be one moment," he says, pointing with two outstretched hands to what appears to be the designated waiting area—two wine-colored leather sofa chairs set about a low, round glass table. It is the design you would find in a car dealership.

Carol wipes her face with a flowered washcloth she keeps in her purse, leans back in the chair. It is an awkward lean and she fights for a moment to return upright, but that pose is difficult and she gives in to the slumping soft leather.

A young female employee makes her way from the back wearing a skirt to her ankles. Carol guesses it to be the daughter. This girl places a glossy-white cardboard box on the wooden counter, forces a smile at Carol and takes a seat on a stool a short distance from her father.

Carol wonders if he, or this girl, has recognized her son's name from the broadcasts and if they have put the information together. This possibility is why she has left Aisha in the car. They were delivered her son's body and the attached paperwork with his cause of death. It is possible this is all they know, she thinks. Boys who simply commit suicide cannot be that uncommon.

The mortician has again put on his reading glasses and is preparing papers behind the counter. The young woman has found a magazine to busy herself.

Carol had discovered Donnie as she lifted the garage open, Aisha in the passenger seat. She does not remember the weight of the wooden garage door or maneuvering to avoid its bottom-heavy ascent. It plays as the noiseless parting of a movie curtain. She did hear the crack of the damaged door of her Civic that she had been meaning to get repaired, then its slam, as Aisha presumably made her way. She has no real memory of what her daughter did or where she went. Logic tells her she was by her side and she has tried to place her there. She remembers holding her son by the knees and the taste of salty skin. Then grabbing him by the waist to take the weight off and sharing the cool polished cement floor with him. This morning she recalled that she was stroking him, his neck, but does not remember if the fibers of the rope had made an indentation. As she sits in the mortuary, she still cannot retrieve any detail of this. But this man, the mortician, would have studied Donnie's body. She wants to apologize for the remark or attitude that has landed her in this uncomfortable seat and ask him to describe the texture of her son's wounds.

The sound of shuffling and straightening papers takes her attention and she sees the mortician walk to the female employee and whisper to her ear. The young girl leaves, first handing him the glossy box, which Carol now understands to contain her son. He comes to join Carol in the waiting area. He perches, straight-backed and easily, on the lip of the sofa chair. Carol does her best to push away from the soft leather and mimic his example. He takes from a manila folder a series of papers for her to sign. He marks each with an "X" and slides them slowly across the glass table top, removing the duplicate copies after she has signed and folding them into an envelope with the mortuary's insignia.

As he passes the last form, he places his palm on her shoulder. She meets his eyes with as much grace and apology as she can, blindly signing the last sheet. She only glances down to confirm the amount and searches her handbag for a paper that she has folded into an envelope and separates new one-hundred-dollar bills.

"Would you like to see the design of the urn you have chosen? It is quite lovely."

He begins to open the box. She stops him, places her hand over his and holds his wrist between her fingers.

There is a long silence between them, her hand still covering his. Finally, "Did you cremate my son?"

She realizes this question can be taken a number of ways and begins to form it again but he interrupts by shaking his head. He replaces the box top and tapes the envelope to the top. "The bodies are processed at another facility," patting the box with both hands, seemingly embarrassed by this admission.

Carol walks with her son's ashes between both palms and her purse in the crook of her arm. The mortician follows her to the door and opens it for her. He sees Aisha in the front seat of the car and waves as he holds the door for her mother. She looks in his direction and then continues to look above his head, away from the glare of the sun.

He searches his pockets for a pack of cigarettes and smokes at the entrance as Carol and Aisha discuss how to arrange the box. Carol wedges it between the two front seats. Aisha protests that the ashes might spill into the box because the parking brake has it sitting at an angle. Carol first ignores her, then after another exchange opens the box to demonstrate, as she had expected, that the ashes are secured in the urn by a small Ziploc freezer bag.

On the highway Carol keeps to the slow lane and Aisha removes her sandals and lets her toes play with the mirror and the wind as she reclines in the seat. Aisha has not eaten since the night before and raises her head to examine a sign advertising numerous fast-food restaurants and a gas station at the next exit. She taps her mother's leg and points to it. Carol veers to the right when the exit comes. She has eaten little more than milk and apples in the five days.

Aisha's preference is In & Out and her mother follows the signage to the drive-thru, only to find it roped off and a man with a tool belt working at the service window. She drives to a parking space in front of the restaurant. Carol removes the taped envelope from atop the box and places it in the glove compartment. She loosens the box from its spot between the two front seats and they walk to one of the shaded patio tables.

"Look like a girl," she says, peeling the hood from her daughter's head. Then, "Something small for me," handing Aisha a folded bill.

Aisha returns with a value meal and pushes the basket of fries to her

14

mother. Carol eats only three and the pickles her daughter has left on a napkin.

When Aisha is done with half her burger, she stuffs the rest in its wrapping and carries it and the tray to the trash. She goes into the doors of the restaurant and returns with a bag, napkins and more containers of ketchup. She dumps the basket of fries in the bag and empties the ketchup, one by one, into it. She licks her fingers, seals the bag with her fist and shakes it.

There are still no news trucks as they turn on to 78th Street. Carol hopes they have moved on to another story. She realizes the apartment's gardener has not come this week and that the lawn has grown past its boundary. Tomorrow, she says to herself, I will borrow a mower from a neighbor.

When they have climbed the steps to their unit, Carol sets the box on the balcony and drags her potted fern to the furthest corner where it will catch more of the afternoon sun. A circle of dirt from water that has passed through the pot has left a stain that she will have to scrub.

Carol goes to the kitchen and pulls a soup spoon from the drawer. She returns to the balcony and makes a couple of digs before she abandons it in the dirt and returns to the kitchen. She looks under the sink as if she might have at some time placed a gardening tool there. She settles for a butter knife and pours a glass of water. She passes Aisha, who has turned on the TV in the front room and is eating what is left of the fries.

Carol uses the knife to soften the soil, stabbing it repeatedly and turning the knife when it has reached a few inches deep. She picks up the spoon and removes the loose dirt, wipes the sweat from her forehead and sits on her shins. She calls for Aisha, startled to find her only a few steps behind her, and instructs her to open the box and remove the bag of ashes.

Carol polishes the spoon as she would her glasses on the fabric of her blouse. Aisha holds the bag open while her mother fills the hole and folds the loose dirt back in place, flattening it with the underside of the spoon. She then pours the water from her glass over the base of the plant. Aisha grabs her mother's hand and mouths a prayer.

They both sit on the top step and look out toward the neighborhood. Aisha's head rests on her mother's shoulder. Carol is playing in a braid that has come loose on her daughter's head. A delivery boy reading from a receipt taped to the top of a paper bag looks up at the two of them and asks if this is 78th Place. Carol points down the block to the cul-de-sac.

15

The Death of Sam Brown

From time to time, little men will come along to find fault with what you have done; to say something could have been done better; that there has been some mistake, some shortcoming; that things are not really managed in the best of all possible manners, in the best of all possible worlds. They will have their say and they will go downstream like bubbles; they will vanish.

Theodore Roosevelt—November 16, 1906
Addressing the white American canal workers in Colón, Republic of Panama

All men will be sailors then, till the sea shall free them

Nina Simone—October 26, 1969
Philharmonic Hall, New York

Kingston, 1917

I can think of only the plain way to say this. I am being visited by a spirit, a dead man from my time in Panama that has run me to the services of an obeahwoman in Riverton. My mother would roll her grave, spit dirt to see that her son has succumbed to this country mess. But my sleep has been peppered with nightmares, leaving me to avoid their possibility altogether by joining the night on this balcony. The sun is low and screaming, but it could slap and kick if it wanted and I would still welcome it.

It began with a simple fire. I had taken a leisurely morning trip to the Post Office to collect a small shipment of rough stones. I returned to my landlord throwing buckets of water to my balcony and on the walls of his own shop below. I count myself lucky that he was there as he has been abandoning his responsibilities on this decaying property where he once attempted to sell imported porcelain goods. He helped me clear the room of ash and that is the last I have seen of him. I do not know if he is gone or merely arrives when I am battling the sun for my misplaced sleep.

I did not take this fire for a serious event. Though my workdesk was destroyed, the balcony singed black in spaces and my bed crippled, I slept in my room that very night with my mattress bare on the floor and a mess of burnt wood heaped in the corner much like it is now. This first vision was from a great distance, a toy swinging from a wooden childlike contraption, a bad night's dream. It was quite easy to convince myself that it was the fumes, the residue of burnt paint and polishing oil. The next night I went to Olive, a woman of the town whom I had often courted with a poorly cut gemstone. But blocks away I began to see his face. I awoke to Olive rubbing my chest with her palm until I came to see her and not him. I may have wet the bed, and it is not lost on me that only a paid woman would smother such humiliation with a version of kindness.

That next morning, with the sleepless nights only just beginning to mount, I returned to the site of the fire where an inspector of some sort, a dirt-brown yam stuffed into a constable's uniform, concluded that a piece of

21

my equipment had caused the fire. Delinquency was his verdict and I would be responsible for all repairs. Repairs that still have not been done, all monies going to my obeahwoman, my landlord and my rum. Soon I might be drinking Black Seal and living off coolie-foot rice and the charities of my neighbours. I put up quite a fuss, with good reason, as none of my tools were capable of starting such a fire. But this yam was not to be talked to. I believe my seemingly kind and disappeared landlord was hiding somewhere across town filling this man's mouth with words. Still fearing to be alone, I gathered two flawed emeralds and sold Olive on the prospect of a week's worth of my company.

For five straight nights he confronted me, Olive attentive by my side. On the sixth, with me sack-eyed and delirious, she made her way in the darkness beyond midnight to the kitchen, her eggplant skin barely distinguishable from the night. Over sour coffee I told her of the man that I saw hanging without a creak or bend from the new wood of the gallows, just the sound of the rope turning with his weight on the square beam. She asked if it was a man I knew. I told her that it was not. But in my dream it is always the seventh hour of his dangling, and he is somehow still alive. His left eye socket empty, his face pummelled by rocks, the blood crystallized and the setting sun feeding it. Along with the rope are the hollowed echoes of grinding teeth. Even awake this noise.

Without blinking Olive pushed her eyes over the brim of her cup and in between short sips said that I was no doubt being haunted and that a Mrs. Welcome was known to have great power. Her brother, once driven mad by the red-eyed rolling calf, had been healed by her. But he was a common man, a night ranger at a sugar plantation in Clarendon, and the red-eyed rolling calf was a children's story told to keep one's picknies indoors after dark. To my mother's horror, my aunt used to sit on my bed and tell my sister and me these stories. But this man I see from the Isthmus is no child's play. I cannot strike at him with a pillow. On the seventh night I awoke with this vision inflicting a physical pain. My insides throbbed in a manner that stole my breath. This sensation destroyed all pretence and at nine that morning I boarded the May Penn tram and walked the riverbank to see this woman.

Twenty-four steps to the front yard and two blocks to Orange before I could board a tram the short distance to the Parade and then another west to Riverton. God bless the Queen, or whomever is responsible for this gift of the electric tram. If I were subjected to the mule routes, the slow jerking of wooden wheels manoeuvering the potholes of Spanish Town Road and the unleaving scent of dung wafting from King Street to my balcony, my sleeplessness would have an entirely new and cruel dimension.

Her simple yard was not nearly as run down as I expected. A pleasant walk along the gully, past the vegetable market and the common toilet, brought me to the now familiar jumble of plants and round red stones in a tended garden of green grass. A worn path leads to a wooden door and a clean cool room that smells of lavender. Her hand always finds mine to guide us to the pair of rocking chairs in the corner. She pours from a kettle that rests on the crooked wooden table that divides us. She always sits with legs crossed beneath a white dress, hands caressing a warm cup. Her way possesses me. She is as old as I would imagine my grandmother to be if she were still alive. Two plaits give the image of well-oiled horns, a docile ram with glowing black skin is the best I could describe. All of her matches the air and when our sessions are over I must sit for a moment feeling the lavender river breeze run through me, wishing to stay there, away from the growing noise of West Kingston, away from the dirty air, and away from him.

It is Monday and I will soon ply myself away from my night watch and this excuse for a grand balcony, pour another drink and begin to prepare for the brief daylight sleep I intend to have before Qua, my neighbour's son, is to wake me for his lessons. I will stand naked in the centre of this room and pour a mixture of oils, garlic and dark-green herb into a puddle in my palm and bathe every reachable crevice. I have been given a peppermint liniment that I will gently massage into my stiffening left wrist then lay down on my mattress to close my eyes and be baked by the morning sun. At near two in the afternoon Qua will knock with rough knuckles. I will produce some noise that will be understood as *one moment*. Naked, I will take that moment to reach onto the balcony, find my chair, my robe, and stumble to a smiling boy with a freshly shaven head and a scar below his half-closed lazy left eye.

My life has been reduced to this ritual.

Qua lives with his mother in the room at the back of a yard that the short side of my balcony overlooks. I rely on the boy for my errands and he on my tutoring. When I had first returned from Panama, to my north was the respectable tenement of a high-brown doctor of medicine. Now, it has been parcelled up with a shack being erected for the boy and his mother in the absent doctor's garden. The doctor has long since rushed east to the comforts and straight leaning houses of Kingston Gardens. She is the baker and her son the fleet-footed delivery boy. The two make a near silent symphony of running, mixing, wrapping. The sound of steel sliding on steel is all that gives their enterprise away. Months ago, in my days of walking about, when my hair and beard were always trim and proper, I would see her shovelling the thick cakes in and out of the stove at all hours of the day. On occasion she would chat me up on my return from an errand, trying to get at (without coming out with it) why a man of my tone had remained when all the rest had not.

Those visits have shown their dividends. She has now developed the custom of sending a bun up with Qua when he comes to run his Monday errand. I am continually surprised at how something so delicate is born out of a place seemingly composed of only dust, twisted boards and heat. I always send down a halfpenny with the boy, walking the length of the balcony to see him deliver it to his mother, watching her open her gap-toothed mouth to me. In this game I always manage a smile and then turn to watch Qua scrabble out of his back gate, arms piled with boxed cakes ready for delivery and my medicine money bulging in the hind pocket of his dust-greyed short pants.

His delivery route takes him as far west as Tower Hill, so it is less than a kilometre for him to travel to the riverbank and on to Mrs. Welcome's. It is a place where, as a kid, I would have been scared to enter, fears and stories of fears, but the boy is none affected. He thinks of it as an adventure, I imagine. In our lessons that always follow the delivery of my medicine, I will ask him about the day's trip. He will tell me about Mrs. Welcome's powders and her stories of the saints. This is how we practise our diction. It is only when he is seated on my floor (I have but one chair) that I require him to use the Queen's English. He will squirm and roll his eyes to prevent himself from reverting to his patois. When he has given up, I prompt him to mimic my answers to the questions. He does this staring straight to my lips, though the muscles of his left eye betray him.

Mrs. Welcome says the fire was his announcement, his way of making sure I was paying attention. And though we have not yet exorcised this spirit, we have solved my stomach. A brew of ginger root and peppermint allows me to eat porridge, Qua's mother's sweet buns and stews, and the grapefruits, mangos and oranges that the higglers rolling their carts to the market are kind enough to toss up over my balcony. I can now manage all this without sparking a bout of incontinence, a problem that has plagued me ever since my return from the Isthmus now nine years ago. (This is far more than a Dr. Sheridan at Victoria Jubilee was able to do. His best guess was to threaten me with the same quinine that was fed to us daily on the canal. That was like swallowing rust, an effort that I could not and will not bear again.) Mrs. Welcome has admitted that the spirit is strong with me and has compelled me to continue my visits. My contributions, as she calls them, have amounted to eight shillings this last month alone. I have sometimes wondered if she is beguiling me, if this is the same she tells all her clients, especially those more well off. What she does not know, or counts on, is that I am more desperate than well off.

It is the evening, the boy lingered and we spoke of sharks. Minutes ago I was watching the sun play tricks with the bottles he has delivered, catching the colours of the herb and returning dulled light to the wall. Monday's bath sits beside my bed and the oils. I have instructed Qua to return in the morning for the spoiled water, though by that time it may only be cold. What do I have to bathe for? The lemon-scented water and coconut soap cower to the garlic of my skin. And, honestly, it is too close to night. Invite him is Mrs. Welcome's instruction. A cruel trick, that in order to extinguish this horror I am to imagine, re-imagine rather, all sides of it.

In my letters to Margaret, the only one I corresponded with while away in Panama, I gave her the impression that Empire was an Eden. I had lived and worked there my last eighteen months on the canal as Mr. Kerr's lapidary and jewelling apprentice and only sent brief letters filled with positive words and remittances as she was settling herself in Georgia.

In 1908, the American section was as elegant as one could expect for a camp a mere mile from the worst of the work on the Isthmus. Empire had been the largest of the French construction towns and the Americans went to great lengths to repair the housing the French had left to sit alongside their own. It was the headquarters to the Central Division and the base for its engineers and higher officials, giving it the largest population of whites in the interior camps.

The Police Station and a low-fenced playing field marked the division between the Americans and the West Indians. It was difficult to give a number to us. The way we were arranged it was like counting a flood of rats. Where the American section contained not only the playing field I have mentioned, but a music hall, a billiards club and other amenities I can only guess at, the section where we slept and ate was bare. This difference was not intended to be subtle. I do recall writing to Margaret of her Americans' clever segregation and tricks of colour: "Gold Roll" for the American and European and "Silver Roll" for the rest. Though there were a few American blacks, the administration had given up on this attempt, found them too unruly and shipped as many as could be found home. Only the meekest or those most indispensable remained.

The silvermen—it is quite ridiculous that I had then grown accustomed to this phrasing—we were connected to the same sewer system as the Americans but a good proportion of our water closets and bath houses were in permanent disrepair. And let us not talk of food, rice that could be used as shot to kill a lion. And where the American bachelors slept two to a room, forty of us, or more in some cases, shared barracks (they called them dormitories) with canvas bunks stacked three to the ceiling. In this case I was fortunate, my dormitory a small converted French house that fit only seven. This was unbearable enough, forty I could not imagine.

A burgeoning municipal sprawl at the border of the American section closest to the Police Station and playing field contained those offices needing access to the railroad: the gold commissary, an administration building that held the post office, a firehouse and a health office from which the quinine men were dispatched with tanks strapped to their back and paper cups. This office is where minor cases of malaria and fever were treated before they were carried to the rest house at Culebra and those more serious to Ancon. The roofs of this section were all of the same red-painted shingles. Of course, in the time of two rainy seasons they had been reduced to only a pinkish hue but still distinctive from the bare mess halls, cook sheds and dormitories of our section just to its south. Part of this sprawl, on the eastern path behind the gold commissary, was my workshed. It overlooked the ridge below which the trains would run carrying the debris from the Cut. It was originally to be a storage shed for the commissary. But Mr. Kerr, my boss, through some favour had made the arrangements. It was small with a stone floor, a modest skylight and no windows, but rose-shingled nonetheless.

Mr. Kerr had come to Empire the second Sunday in December to bring more work and the tools I had asked for weeks before. I thought he would give his instruction and leave, carry on up the road to the offices of the high officials as was his custom, but he arranged the stools at the mouth of my workshed and asked for me to sit with him. I offered the sweetened tea I had brewed at the cookshed for my Sunday work, cleaned the glasses with a rag as my back was turned. I thought he might be anxious to discuss the explosion at Bas Obispo the day before. It had been the biggest on the Isthmus and quite a controversy already, the papers had one report, the men another. Or, I thought he might speak of the fact that the Isthmian Canal Commission was constructing gallows for a man they were to hang the following Saturday just beyond the playing field. The manner in which our chairs were arranged we stared directly at this. But of either he said nothing. He sipped his tea, the tension visible in his shoulders as he perched himself on the stool. I wondered, in fact, if he was aware of what he was looking at. The gallows project that morning was incomplete, two barrel-sized pillars sticking straight to the air and a small wooden stage.

I remember sitting in the silence waiting for him to speak. The fresh shine that he had put to his shoes had collected the red clay dust known to the camp at Empire. He wore a tight-fitting dark suit that gathered up his shins as he sat, showing monogrammed socks pulled tight. Despite his clothes, he did not sweat.

27

The commissary's delivery boy, whom I had often used to run errands on my behalf, a creamy-skinned Barbadian, stood at a tree some yards off aiming rocks over the ledge at the rails. I was aware that I was allowed certain things (the indoor work, &c.), but the boy shot looks at me as if I had crossed a line—the sight of this coloured man having an afternoon tea with this white man and his clean dark suit. Had Mr. Kerr caught me looking at the boy? He even turned in that direction, but looked through the boy, to the field where a collection of white men was playing the Americans' baseball.

"Are you a fan?" he asked. "Of the sport?"

"It's no more than a crippled adoption of our rounders," I said and he put out a short laugh but returned to sip from his tea. The conversation dropped and, embarrassed, I resolved to say not another witty remark. He only stared out at the field, unaffected by the short four-car train that passed noisily below the ridge. The men in the field did not take notice either. They continued to shout, swinging at a ball with their minuscule bats. If not for the same conductor, whose greased and sun-bleached moustache was familiar even from my distance, I would have taken his tarped loads to be other things, rocks. But I was unsure. He had passed in either direction at least eight times since the explosion, carrying the injured and the dead, and was now racing the afternoon sun back to Ancon to be through with his assignments.

I was caught again by the discomfort of the boy following my gaze as my eyes followed the train. Mr. Kerr began to speak. In my anxiety with the boy and my muddled thoughts of the train and its collection of bodies or rocks, I did not hear his statement from the beginning. When I returned to him, he was not looking at me but at the gallows and was discussing how he would like me to cut the bloodstone he had delivered. He brought with him a diagram and I fingered it.

"It should not be too difficult," he said.

"I will work by lamp into the night if I have to," assuring him that he would have it by the next day's five o'clock train.

Of a sudden, propelled by one strong breath, he stood.

"You are not like the others, Brown," patting my back as he set down his glass and excused himself to return to Panama City. This name, Brown, was what I went by on the Isthmus. I had invented it on the boat trip over. It was for me a new beginning. If one were to ask for Sam Lawson, they would not find me. I was Sam Brown.

That was not the first time he had come to Empire to bring me work on a Sunday, but it was the first time he had invited me to sit with him and that we had talked of such things as baseball. I was another man in his presence. When I reached to hand him the tea I had poured, I found myself explaining that the water had been twice boiled and sweetened with sugar bought from the commissary, not a peddler. And these jokes about this foolish sport—*our rounders?* Mr. Kerr pretended to believe (or foolishly believed, I am still not sure) that in Kingston I spent my weekends playing this silly game, not fetching salt and groceries for Mrs. Virgil, my aunt's boss before she passed. I was not too many months removed from the task of carrying wheel barrows of explosives in the jungles. I had, when I was first recruited by Mr. Kerr, thought of myself as a jeweller's apprentice, but that was not true. I ground the stones he delivered in simple cuts, was not allowed to do more. The illusion that I would learn the trade was slowly dying in me, I simply wished to be through with the Isthmus. To return home, or maybe go to Georgia with Margaret, with fuller pockets before the next rainy season began, though I did not know how any of this could or would occur.

It was the shameful prospect of failing in this ambition that frightened me most of all. Some of the workers would return home, flaunt their entire savings in a month and then stow away once more as if this is what they had intended. And there were the pragmatic among us who fessed about the realities of this world and returned with their wives and built a life. I had no woman to speak of and knew I was neither capable of pragmatism nor possessing the carefree spirit to return penniless.

After Mr. Kerr left, I spent the whole morning procrastinating. I counted the passing trains, wondering which were headed east to gather and carry more dead to Monkey Hill, the cemetery near Colón where the blacks were buried. The afternoon rains called me inside and I began to cement the bloodstone to the closed end of my steel pipe. Once it was set, I would begin the polishing work Mr. Kerr had assigned me.

The rainy seasons of the Isthmus were not the hurricane rains of my childhood. The violence of those winds also spelled relief—soon this will blow by. If it were hail, Noah, the Virgil's young boy, Margaret and I would wait for a break and collect the balls of ice and have my aunt pour lemon and sugar to them. The rains of the Isthmus were a different matter. They sat on you without regard for progress. It was the only time I would invoke the word of

God in anything resembling prayer. But those final efforts of the rainy season were playful and did not last more than the noon hour and so I sat with my tool moulding the bloodstone with my thumb around the cool cylinder measuring the world I had found myself in.

A quarter mile to the south in a burst of wet sunlight a squat man was securing the crossbeam of the new gallows. The trains continued to speed along the tracks in the rain. At each passing, the instructional drawings I had nailed to the wooden planks of my workshed shook their curled edges. A white woman, solid legged and with curls of auburn, caught in the predictable storm, passed with her veil pulled against the rain. Her shoes and stockings would be near red with the mud of Empire by the time she returned from her errand. She was headed to the gold commissary directly behind my workshed. This was not an uncommon sight—at the noon hour the gold commissary served the sprinkling of resolute and soiled wives of the decorated gold employees who had braved the small storms to buy meats and sweets for their husbands while the camp's blacks had disappeared to the jungled hills to work for their silver. As this woman neared the entrance to my shed, because this is where the path was most navigable, I waved and may have even spoken, but she only looked down. This was not always the case. Some would speak as they passed, some even without any provocation. The next day, or the day after, these delicate outfits would be clean and the sun-dried women would repeat this determined stroll.

The whites, in any significant quantity, had been a new arrival to Empire, coming only after the commission had refurbished their living quarters. Now near to seven hundred lived in spacious homes off the cul-de-sac of the one paved road and in the surrounding manicured foothills. At this stage, servants were hard to keep, most preferring the independent city life of Colón, washing the clothes of the bachelors in the tenements or opening salons. There was one, a Mrs. Mary, with whom I would fruitlessly flirt. To my disappointment, her sister had found her a job at the sanitarium in Miraflores and she had left three weeks before.

These American whites were a mystery to me. With the blacks it was clear my handle, my lever, was the mystery of me, my silence. As meek as this may appear (and no matter the amount of childish insults that I endured from the men in my dormitory), the fact that I was there yet set apart in my workshed was a saving grace for me. Though our conversations never approached a subject of any great seriousness, there was a strong and resounding fear or interest in what I was thinking, doing in all this time away. But my interaction with the whites, even in the casual sense, as with the woman who passed my shed that morning, was quite different. I am not entirely sure I can identify it, and this may have been an undoing of sorts.

The foot pedal turned without its usual creak as I had put to it the oil Mr. Kerr had brought. In my concentration, I took Robert's soggy steps on the footpath to be thicker raindrops. I was surprised to see my friend's face rippling from his smiling mouth. A hat, curled on the sides, covered a full head of matted hair, his pipe sitting in the space of a missing front tooth. We embraced, the droplets of warm rain jumping from his oilskin covering to my shoulders and back. I poured rum from a bottle I kept beneath my workdesk and sat opposite him at the edges of my shelter, the rain blowing through the door onto my boot. "No use for an old man today?" I said.

"They'd steal my last breath if I let 'em." He pitched his head back and took the entire glass in one swallow. I filled his again. "I have given the men the day off," he said. He took a smaller sip and then set the glass on the uneven ground to lift his rain covering and get at a tobacco pouch to fill his pipe. "You remember Fifty-nine?"

"Yes," I said smiling—his nickname, 11:59, coming because his skin was that close to midnight.

"He's dead." Robert said this balancing the pipe on his lips and then paused to light it, sucking in three rapid breaths that showed the lean muscles of his face. "I sent him to bring fuses to the shop in Bas Obispo."

He said no more. I was to understand that he felt responsible for his death, that he had marched him there. "Are you sure?" I said.

"I come from there."

There was no pattering on the roof of my shed, the cloud had emptied itself or moved away to a direction we could not see. He asked if I had read the day's *Star and Herald*, though he knew it was my daily habit. Robert spoke Spanish, the English he used with me, and patois he used with most of the men, and knew everything there was to know about explosives, a great deal about the geology of the region, yet could not read. I took this as an invitation to read for him the article on the explosion.

"How many they say dead?"

"They are unsure." I read to him again the paragraph that chronicled the activity of the trains carrying the injured.

"They will not say. The officer says it is lightning that set the charge." His pipe glowed and he let out a forced, smoke-filled laugh. "I saw no cloud in the sky. You?"

The explosion was at eight in the morning, the clouds of that December did not come before noon. I shook my head in agreement.

"Did you hear the blast?" he asked.

"I thought it to be normal, until the trains."

He hesitated in lighting his pipe as if he might speak. A train passed with three cars carrying mounds of earth.

"I first saw the trains with the injured, the dead came shortly after, even today," I told him. Two blacks walked up the slope by the rails and acknowledged us with a wave.

"Only reason there's a fuss, because more than one going that way," he said, pointing his pipe toward Ancon where the whites were buried. A milky puddle rested on the bottom lid of his left eye and would not break. "I saw them stack Fifty-nine on the dump car with the rest while the white boys go neatly in the pine box."

The previous night the men in the dormitory had talked long past curfew about the two men who had yet to return. Just then I could not help imagining their bodies stacked like logs alongside Fifty-nine and being taken to Monkey Hill. I had listened for a while and then used their ignorance of the curfew imposed in the dorms to keep a candle burning and read from my book.

"The foreman say they will get proper burial. I sent a man to see. Mr. Strong tried to give a fight." Robert was Mr. Strong's strawboss, his second in command.

Robert sucked again from his pipe and continued. "I once saw a pole go right through a man's skull. Standing right next to me…" He had begun this same story this same way each of the two previous times he had told it. The first time was within a week of my apprenticeship with him in the explosive shop. It was told in a jovial manner and passed the time as I learned the explosives I was soon to cart to the men in the Cut. The second was after a member of another crew had foolishly leapt from a detaching railcar and in his misjudgement fell to the tracks and was split in half by the car he had just leapt from. He laughed in this telling, but with a cautionary tone.

32

"One minute he telling lies about a woman he have back home and the next a pole fell from the scaffold and clear cut his skull. He fell to the ground but wasn't dead. His eyes blinked and the poor man couldn't even talk if he wanted the last word. And just like that the man stop blinking. I turned him on his back, the pole went all the way to here." He pointed to the roof of his mouth, sticking his finger two knuckles deep as he had done each time before.

"As far as I know, they bury'im pole and all. Until now, the worst I seen. Even when the men were falling from the fever with the French. They'd twirl in a spot when they had it real good and fall out right there. Each day you see that. Most of the men would not come back from the rest houses those days."

This bit about the French was new, he had spoken only briefly about this time in his life. "How are the men?" I asked, but he was caught in his distant moment. "How are they feeling?" I added as I stood to break his trance and refill his glass.

He wiped at his eye before he sipped. "Weary. Even before news of Fifty-nine. Sam, it's a boxing match and our back's on the ground. Each step we take the hill fall right back." He smacked his palm against his wet trousers to mimic falling rocks. "The number of dead will be high, higher than they are saying," pointing to the paper. "I seen it with my eyes."

I stood and walked toward the open door and looked out. The rain had stopped and it was not merely a break in the cloud. We left my shed for a walk, as we had always done in his visits to Empire. If I am to be honest, there was a sense of display that I enjoyed, this old timer and I in intimate conversation. He handed me his pipe and removed his oilskin. We walked down the slope by my shed, past the tree where the boy had been staring, and began to follow the ridge to the gallows. Beyond the gallows, beyond the silver camps, where the clouds had run, was the Empire Cut, then Culebra. Culebra was too far off to be seen, but the explosions were audible and ongoing, even on a Sunday. I held the pipe awkwardly in my palm, careful not to tip the bowl. I imagine like a boy would hold his father's. It was bleached wood, worn black in the groove where his thumb rested, a gentleman's pipe that had found its way to the heart of the Isthmus. When the French had retreated, they had left quickly and wanted nothing that reminded them of this place. In that way, the pipe was a gift. He reached for it back and cupped it in his hand effortlessly as he ambled alongside me toward the gallows.

"We remember him tomorrow at sunset," he said. "I want you to read something from the Book."

"And they have given you the evening off?"

"We will remember our dead when they die." He continued, "Mr. Strong won't fuss, because the white boys died."

"I am to present my work to Mr. Kerr in the City in the evening."

"When you finish."

It was settled. We walked by the playing field. I palmed each post of the boundary as we passed it. The men and their bats were gone, a worker from the commissary storeroom sent out after the rain to chalk the field again. He was deaf and walked with his back hunched pouring from a paper sack a white line on top of the outline that was nearly washed away by the short storm. A train passed. It was again tarped. It was either returning to Monkey Hill with the black bodies of the injured who had succumbed to their wounds in the hospital at Ancon, or it was back to hauling dirt and had been covered for the noonday rains. Had the deaf man felt its rumble? I assumed that he had lost his hearing in an explosion and had been reclassified. It was not uncommon, one-armed men turned to parcel deliverers. But maybe he was fortunate enough to have come like this.

"If you were to be removed a sense and placed again on the Isthmus, what would it be?" I asked Robert. "Surely it would be my hearing," staring at the man in the field.

"Smell," as if he had already spent long hours arriving at the conclusion. "The food be much better and I wouldn't have to come here to get the lead out my nose." He took a breath of the wet air and turned to me with a grin. "You think I walk to see you?"

"On a day like today I could look toward the green trees, away from the construction of the gallows and not be battered by the sound of explosions. I could be much more effective in my daydreaming. A sleep without the insistent hissing of the insects."

We made it to the wooden stage where in less than one week's time a man was to be led to his death, made to stand on a crate and face the gathering crowd as an Isthmian official kicked the support from beneath him. We sat at the edge of the gallows' frame.

"The paper says the man they are going to kill murdered a woman's husband," I said, gesturing to the gallows above. "Is he not in Culebra jail?"

He shrugged and struck a match. "Only janitor and fool go there."

"But you think it right to hang a man—here?" I asked. Again, it was the same lazy shrug. Though he seemed irritated by the subject of the condemned man, I still pressed the conversation in this direction. It had been on my mind since I had read of it in the paper and I thought it might be a distraction. "If he killed a man, doesn't that seem like justice?"

"And if not?"

"If not what?"

"If he did not kill the man?"

He was indifferent, or wished to appear to be, opening the pouch on his lap to pack his pipe once more. I stood to punctuate the point I was forming in my head and realised I had drunk too quickly and on an empty stomach. I regained my balance by leaning on the enormous oak-barreled pole that shot up out of the ground. "Why would I believe them to lie about—that?" I asked. I looked up in amazement at the height and sturdiness of the structure. Had they gone to these lengths for one man?

"You've been locked inside your shed too long." His mood, no doubt set off by Fifty-nine, was responsible for such an honest quip. But it struck in a way that I could not let pass. He pulled me down by the arm and settled me next to him, apologizing in his way. "You forget we live in a strange place—lightning is there and not. And the dead are not dead."

"That is a different matter." I spoke this loudly and picked up the paper I had been reading for him. In his face I saw an apology still unfolding. I lowered my voice. "These papers go to the United States. They must look like they know what they are doing."

He started to search his pockets. In the time since I had left him in Culebra, come to Empire to work for Mr. Kerr, Robert had aged much, or I was seeing with new eyes. In the past, it was only his laugh that showed his wrinkles and missing tooth. His skin now had a layer of grey and his eyes leaked uncontrollably. When I first arrived, giddy at the thought of proving myself a man, Robert, who had been there since my Uncle Jeffrey had come with the French, was a massive presence to me. Now his body was shrunken, lost in his clothes as he reached deep in his pocket to find a handkerchief.

After a long silence, "Do you think it wrong that I have taken on so long with Mr. Kerr?"

He first looked at me as if he would disregard my question.

"You are a son to me." He had circled my point and like a child I jabbed at the dirt with the toe of my boot. "There's a way that passed you by—stares you in the face out there."

"I was out there," I said.

"One short season. It did not stick."

"And has it always been *this* way? With the French, too?"

"Different ways—but yes."

"Then why have you not returned home?"

"I came same as you, to earn money and return. I had a pregnant wife. I have told you the story." He drew from the pipe, sucking too deeply, and began to choke but continued. "That is gone. If I leave now, I leave a hole in the ground. Work my life for a hole?"

"I'm a young man. Do you expect me to grow old waiting for this hole to be finished?"

"No." He began to fold the handkerchief over in his hand but turned to me and let the eye leak into the wrinkles of his face.

"It is not yet time. I have provided for Margaret, but what do I show for myself?"

"More than these men," pointing at the paper that was still curled in my fist. "It is safer in there," looking back toward my workshed, "but it is still no place for a man to spend his life." I fingered the deck of the stage between my thighs. "It smells of your time," he said. "You think it always is like this but it'll soon disappear."

He spoke about a friend who could arrange my exit papers, a man who worked the steam shovels when I was with him in Culebra. "Do you remember him?" he asked.

Now it was me who gave a shrug.

We walked the distance to the shed in silence, the thought of my departure between us as we pulled the stools outside and stared at the sky that had lost its silver-blue to announce its evening. My stomach gave a painful turn and I remembered again that I had not eaten. I stood and left the shed without a word, crossed the camp's centre to my dormitory and took from my storage shelf a package of dried meats. We ate as lines of workers returned, following the tracks. "Never so many on a Sunday," he said.

"They brag in the paper of how well it is going. It is us that have to make it true," feeling as if a peace had been made. I looked toward the empty playing field and asked if similar men were preparing for a match in Culebra as well. He smiled. "They must find something they can win." He threw a bone out of the shed and told me he used to be a very good batsman when he played cricket in the road as a boy. "Wicked," he said. "Any stick you give, even the thin one, you won't get it by me."

If it had been earlier, or a different moment perhaps, I would have taken him on his challenge, had the creamy-skinned boy find us a proper bat and some old cans to make a game, shown the boy I was not so bad and found the real smile of my friend.

We had finished the rum and between long pauses his eyes closed. Soon he was asleep. I took a blanket from beneath my worktable and covered him and closed the door. My work could wait until the morning, though I took Mr. Kerr's diagram to study before bed.

My bowels stirred me awake. I found my boots and left the snoring men behind. The trains had stopped, the explosions as well. Even the grey light had quieted most of the insects, the birds only just beginning to start. On the path I squinted and saw that the door to my workshed was open, the blanket folded over the chair and the empty glasses stacked one within the other on the table. It was better this way, I thought, and made a penguined run to the latrine in my nightclothes and untied boots.

I squatted at the raised concrete hole, cataloguing what I had taken in since the explosion. Yucca chips from the vendors and the dried meat I had shared with Robert, rum and tea. No boiled water, no fruit, and not a single proper meal in the mess hall. There was a cracking noise from an insect in the stall. With my sleeping pants about my ankles, I stretched forward to unhinge the door and let the light in. It was a small bug without colours, only frightened and with a voice much larger than its dimension.

I rose from my squat to rest, to rub my belly and coax things out. I wiped my forehead and came away with sweat, the same with my neck and beneath my shirt. The urge came again, but still nothing. This dance continued for what I imagined to be at least a half hour, a brighter light showing through the cracks, the footsteps of men. A pain began. Every natural sensation in my body was moving me to push, but my resolve would not translate and I clenched my teeth to avoid a scream. I reached to feel, hoping my mind had played it larger, but a mound had swelled and a browned blood ran down the back of my leg. I could, again, no longer sit. A man approached and knocked, pulled at the door. Minutes later there was a second knock. "Man, what take so long!" this one said. I hissed him away to the stalls on the opposite end of the camp. There were other knocks. If they knew it was the jeweller's apprentice whom they often teased with their jealous insults, would they have gathered and rocked the stall from all sides? I moved to the filthy ground and arranged myself on my knees and forearms, not yet accepting that unless I walked about town on my hands or crawled in this position I was only delaying the inevitable.

Soon the knocks stopped and it occurred to me that, when I was done with it, I would be forced to walk back to the dormitory in my nightclothes while all others were fully dressed, scattering to their duties. I sat again, my body tired of my hesitations and working on its own, slowly ripping skin. I reached my hand back and found my finger, of its own accord, digging out a hole in what had been exposed. I addressed my rogue finger with a curse, but when two pieces fell into the toilet I reacted like a madman, inserting and pulling until it was only liquid and blood and then I returned to my knees, then rolled over on my side.

Only shame forced me to stand with legs I could not straighten to wipe my fingers with the paper. I gathered more, balled it and gingerly placed it between my legs to catch what dribbled as I walked. I rubbed dirt on my pants so the stains would not be so obvious and crossed the square. It was bright to me because I had left in the dark but it was not yet past morning as I had expected. Many workers were still in the camp, pulling on hats and walking with loosely tied boots as they left their rooms. One remained in our dormitory. I regarded him and stood about the side of my bed. He looked at my nightclothes but did not say a thing. As a rule, the six men that I had shared that space with had stopped in their trying to figure me. My outfit was merely to be one more piece to my ongoing mystery. He made conversation and I busied myself with the laying of clothes I would wear that day and even arranged my toiletry shelf twice in order to avoid sitting down and embarrassing myself with the task.

He left and I fell on the bed, took my clothes off and covered myself with the sheet.

I slept deeply for some two hours before I set to finish Mr. Kerr's tasks, uncaring if the Zone Police banged down the door in their periodic bed checks and hauled me to jail for being in camp during work hours. If they came, I told myself, I would limply let them take me away and continue my sleep wherever they dropped me.

When I finished the gemstone, I rode the back of a labour train to Panama City to hand-deliver it to Mr. Kerr. Beyond the sensation of leaking, the pain of the morning had only made me walk slower. It was nearing five o'clock and Mr. Kerr was expecting me.

"Would you like a sweet roll?" he asked as I entered.

I waved my hand, content to only drink for the next days. He poured juice from a pitcher and put a glass in front of each of us.

"I have a local woman who brings me this each afternoon," he said. "Agua de Piña. If it weren't for the mosquitoes and the dynamite, this place would be a paradise." After a pause, "This is what the wife says."

I had no witty response. I had left soiled nightclothes in a paper sack at the foot of my bed. "Your wife is here now?" I asked, feigning interest as I sipped from the glass.

"No. These are only my complaints in my correspondence with her. When things have settled and business has built up, she and my daughter will come."

I did not ask more of his family. I took from my pocket the stone, unfolded it from its felt rag and slid it across the mirrored table. I only wanted to be done with the errand. Mr. Kerr examined the stone, first on the table, then holding it to his eye.

"Have they finished with the gallows?" he asked.

"They seem to be done. The workers did not come today."

He made some joke about the hanging man. I did not laugh.

"The Warden thinks it important for them to be a visible structure."

Again, I had no response.

"I have met with the General, the one this stone is to be for. There is some concern for how the workers will react to the hanging of the murderer. It is what is left of the American negroes that grab their concern."

He set his glass on the table and squared his eyes to mine. I was to speak.

"He is a murderer. If it is just, it is just," I said.

"This General is not so relaxed. He is looking for assurances. In fact, I have told him about you. I have told him that I have a man in Empire."

"And what have you told him?"

"The truth. That you are a man of influence."

"I'm not sure of what influence you are speaking."

"You have your ear in many rooms, Brown. This could be of great help." He stood and returned to the glass counter where he displayed his finer jewels and watches. "I see you have been selling stones to the men?"

Did he pay the curious creamy-skinned boy for such information?

"I polish what they bring from the ditches," I said. "In my spare time."

"I have no quarrel with this. I see in you a man of great ambition—have seen it from the start. And how has this venture gone?"

"Since the rain has lessened, on my day off I have been walking the ruins myself and selling what I find as well. The men have been finding animal teeth off Paraiso. I tell them they are from the ancient sharks though I don't know."

40

"And the money?"

"It has been small."

"But they must talk to you, and not in the way they would talk to me or an officer."

"Yes." I was not entirely sure this was correct, but this was the answer he wanted and so the answer I gave.

"I will give you more for this private business, not just the moonstone they bring. A new site has been discovered and I have a surplus of stones."

"And what am I to give you?"

"I only want information. If you are to hear anything. We have the police but they are as corrupt a lot as any and, like I have said, these generals are looking for assurances. The press of the explosion did not look good. The last they want to see is that they have lost control."

"Will this arrangement continue? After the man is dead?"

"Straight to the guts of it," laughing. "These are men you wish to have on your side."

It would be a lie if I claimed to be unaware of where a conversation of this sort could lead.

"I want a better wheel and the chance to learn the more sophisticated faceting," I said.

He breathed in this last request and I forced myself to keep my eyes upon his face. He turned away and I looked down at the mirrored table where his veined hands surrounded the glass of juice.

"Come by in the morning and we will see what kind of help you can be. This last visit to Empire I meant to bring this up, but the time passed and, well, we were distracted by other things."

I remained on the train as it passed Culebra. My intention was to return to the service where I was expected to read after I had taken a brief rest and thought over what had just occurred. The men were no doubt gambling and shouting in the dormitory and I continued on to my shed. I picked up the paper that I had left, trying to read on the instability in Haiti but it was gibberish in my state. Sitting most of the day had taken its toll. I laid the blanket that had covered Robert, folded it twice to pad the hard floor and held my hands together above my head, feeling the tension in my body begin to sink. Through the slats I could see the gallows. It struck me, in a way that it had yet to, that a man would soon hang from them.

It was deep night when I awoke, the service of Fifty-nine long over. Curled on my side with the newspaper as a pillow, my nails itched through my trousers at a series of bites on my shin. I returned to the dormitory unnoticed by the Zone Police or the loudly sleeping men.

I did not bathe, only wet my head at the stand-pipe and fixed my hair in place with mineral oil and rode the rear of the first train through camp. Soon Mr. Kerr arrived looking entirely out of place with a black pinstripe suit and small-knotted tie.

"Did you arrive with the sun?" he asked while searching his pockets for the keys to the shop.

"I've just arrived," I told him as he opened the door and walked to the rear to hang his coat.

"I see you have no bag," he said. "If you are to be a true man of the trade you need a proper bag." He disappeared into a closet and returned with a brown leather satchel and a folded newspaper. "It's been beneath stacked boxes and has lost its shape." He began to open it and bend out the creases before he handed it and the newspaper to me.

I asked what we were to do.

"The newspaper," grabbing it from me. He peeled a single sheet and balled it and shoved it into a bottom corner of the bag. "Have you just woken, boy?" I took the newspaper and repeated this until the bag was bulging.

"There's an American grocer down the street. Tell him you are picking up for me. And bring us some bananas and coffee." He handed me a coin and turned away.

The grocer was setting up. He was thin, old and white and walked with his shoulders pointing to the ground. He had been brought here to cater to the Americans and regarded me as if he was about to ask a question but did not. "I work for Mr. Kerr," I said, adding, "the jeweller," as he continued to stare at me. I pointed across the street and then handed him a silver coin and instructed him to give me a bunch of bananas and two mugs of coffee. He squinted in the direction I had pointed and then looked back to me, examining my outfit. It was not a suit, but was he surprised to see a clean shirt and trousers at an hour when most would be dirty with the jungle? He took the coin after I had set it on the table.

I took one of the stools that sat under the overhang and began to eat a banana and stare out at the street. I sensed his eyes upon me as he set up the pot and scuttled about, fixing up the minute storefront. I had made a vow to not eat until the following day, but I was starved and feeling better. The sun had yet to burn and the crowds had yet to arrive. I could slightly see the paradise that men like Mr. Kerr had begun to imagine. It was a different world than the camps. The lush green jungle that surrounded the wide and cleanly paved corridors of this section of the city that was full of the American influence did not appear menacing but enchanting. And the smell of the ocean cut through those corridors. In Empire, the jungle was never ending and the ocean a rumor. Even the local colour, though just blocks away, seemed miles off, and one had the impression that they were disappearing themselves as you stood. I had been to the city on several occasions, to this exact street, but had never before seen this developing reality with such simplicity. I was overtaken and thought of Robert. To him was it really, as he had said, only the hole and no more? Could he even see such promised land?

I looked to Mr. Kerr's shop with its gold-lined letters written on glass. It was the germ of the idea that the Americans had come to Panama to announce—there would be no immunity from their version of progress. And though my workspace was only a converted storehouse in the midst of the cheap and impermanent architecture of the camps, it was a fragment of this same germ. In that moment, I felt fortunate to have my work with Mr. Kerr and my position on the Isthmus.

I was drunk with the flavour of the banana and the early morning sun. I turned to the counter to reach for another from the bunch, but the nasty old man had placed them in a paper sack and was standing with the two mugs. I slapped the peel on the counter with unnecessary force, knowing he had not placed my relationship to Mr. Kerr and was hesitant to run me away with foul words and his broom as may have been his desire.

We finished breakfast then carried the grinding wheel to the table. It had the weight of an elephant. Our faces were inches apart and we walked in small awkward steps to avoid crossing our feet.

"He is a funny old man—the grocer." I spoke with my mouth pointing away from his.

His shoulders were straining with the massive wheel and he waited until it was set on the table before he exhaled deeply. "He can be an evil bugger. You must have caught him on a good morning."

"How does a man so old end up here?"

"I've decided he is the relative of an administrator. These permits are not easy to come by."

Mr. Kerr wiped his forehead with a handkerchief and took leave to unlock the case where his stones were kept. He returned to my temporary workdesk with several in a ceramic bowl and instructed me on how I was to polish. I was unsure if the stones were for my business or if I was merely doing his work.

A firm round man walking awkwardly with a cane came to the door of the shop. He was more appropriately dressed than Mr. Kerr, as he had the linen suit and the wide-brimmed straw hat of the Americans. Mr. Kerr immediately left to speak with him. The man took his hat off and played it like a tambourine against the side of his leg. Mr. Kerr turned to point at me and I looked down to my work. There was no laughter between them. Mr. Kerr straightened his posture and the visitor left. He returned bothered and I did not speak.

Of a sudden, when I thought he had disappeared from the front, hunting in the back for something else, he blurted, "These men do not know how business is done. They come with no understanding."

I continued with the wheel. He moved a bottle of lubricant and sat facing me, his elbows on my worktable. The day before he sat at the same table, erect and sipping from his juice. Now he slumped, head in his hands. His eyes, which at first glance looked only slightly sunken, in the reflection of the glass-top table were inhumanly recessed.

"Who was that man?"

"It was the Warden. He has come to see if you have done your job." He looked away and for the first time in our conversations I understood him as honest.

"He looked unhappy at your explanation."

"He's a loon. He twitches so, which is good, I suppose—the poor bastard would drown himself in his own pool of sweat if he could manage to stay in the same place."

He laughed at his joke and I joined him.

"I shouldn't have said that, a good man. He thought he would come to the tropics and retire. The animals here have driven him mad."

"What does he expect me to have done?"

"This is the bulldogging I was referring to. He is a policeman. By nature he is impatient." The monstrosity of the grinding wheel hid my eyes from him.

He was muttering again and turned from me to face the mirror and comb his hair straight with his fingers. "Everything is a favour, Brown."

He spoke as if I could not understand this equation. I would not have been there, in Panama, at his desk, if it were not for an exchange. I cannot think of a moment where I was not aware of the bargain. It was he who seemed crushed by the sudden weight of this awareness, though I dared not even hint at this.

"The good Warden has arranged for the permits that allow me to collect the stones from the canal, that have allowed me to hire you from the commission."

"But it has worked out for you," I said.

"It has. I decorate his guests from home, but now he is nervous. He thinks the workers will use any small excuse to disrupt order. I cannot say I disagree, but he mustn't lose his head, it is contagious."

We dallied over the stone I was to cut, but he was not of the mind to instruct and eventually excused me to return and start fresh the next day.

Mr. Kerr had the illusion that I could influence these men. Other than with those that I sold the stones, my only conversations were with Robert—and he, even, was turning a stubborn old man beyond my influence. But something in me was able to pretend, to hope, and I was able to go along. Mr. Kerr had advanced me my coins for the week and in my pockets I carried five stones that he had given me to trade for their secrets. I had bartered for this fantastic exchange and almost immediately knew it was much more than I could offer.

I did not return the mugs. I knew it was the grocer's intention for me to do so, but I ignored it and Mr. Kerr was in no state to prompt me. It was late afternoon. The streets were in a bright shadow, the sun lost behind the shops. That particular corridor had lost the magic of the morning, or I was sobered by the thoughts I carried.

I entered my rectangled dormitory. The men had returned from work and were again huddled around an empty bunk, gambling. It was a moment before I realised that one of the two men thought dead in the explosion was among them. When I inquired, I was told he merely lost his job and moved to Colón and was back to collect his belongings. When the occasion arose, like this particular one, and I carried through with my determination to talk with the men I shared my sleeping quarters with, their responses would be as disregarding as possible and the exchange was usually left to less than three sentences, sometimes a word. But the men began to chide him, counting the jobs for me he had lost in his few months on the Isthmus. Ultimately, his woman had found him work cleaning the ships that came into dock.

Greg, a Barbadian who had arrived in the dormitory the same week I had and who worked as a member of the drilling gang in Empire Cut, sat shirtless and staring with his elbows propped on the thin metal bar at the head of the bed. I imagined he was gauging whether I would continue to interrupt their game with my conversation or retire to my cot and place my book before me.

I was overcome by a boldness and pulled a small bottle of rum from beneath my bed to share with them. The men were wordless. It was Greg who in all things was their ringleader but he, too, remained silent. It was the man who witnessed my fouled clothes the morning before who did not speak but slid down on the bench he had occupied and offered a seat.

I do not remember the names of the other men. They were playing a poker that I was familiar with, though I feigned ignorance. As the bottle passed, I paid close attention to the hands. They explained that it was a four-card brag with both the two of spades and clubs as the holder's choice, a version of the game I played with Noah on the floor of his bedroom or in the playroom before Mrs. Virgil proclaimed that Kingston was not fit for her boy and he was shipped to England for his secondary education. Panama Black was what the rounded man who sat to Greg's right called it. I watched for two more hands before accepting an invitation to be dealt in.

Soon the voices of the men flowed as I had heard on my approach to the dormitory. The one who had returned to collect his things went on a run and hoarded the lion's share of the coins. We began to play for the goods left behind from the lone man that was thought to have perished. I held a running flush, my first good hand, and sat through Greg's animated bluff. The hand I won was for the man's hat, one of the few things that has come with me from Panama. I placed it on my head and suddenly had a clearer memory of the man who wore it. He was from St. Lucia, the only one in the group that was not related to Greg in some way, quiet and always out with the women, very clean. This was his evening hat. It had not been worn as a shade hat during work and lingered with the scent of musk he would rub behind his ears as he walked past my bunk for his nocturnal romps. Unlike the other men, he was always sober and light-footed. I was, in that moment, ashamed that I had never taken the time to speak with him.

I was careful to drink very little, and let that little sit on my tongue.

Greg looked up at me as he took a long drink, holding the bottle loosely from the neck. His eyes were now in a tired squint. "You have a girlfriend?"

I blushed in surprise.

"You probably have women in and out that shed. The commissary girl? Mrs. Mary?" At the mention of Mrs. Mary I gave an uncontrollable and telling smile. But he was drunk and laughing heartily at his interrogation.

"I could never be unfaithful to your mother." I had thought this thought and in the same instance it had left my lips. It was only a slight variation of the banter I had been forced to listen to each night. One dropped his cards and fell off the bench cackling.

Greg seemed to be searching for something to say. I would be beaten or they would accept me. I laid my hand, although it was a mix and seven was my highest card. I pressed the cards firmly to the table with my fingers to conceal their tremor and looked up to Greg shaking his head with his lips hugging his teeth and the other men joining the fallen man in his bellyache.

Greg's was the top hand and he took the St. Lucian's work boots. Now all of the missing man's items were gone and it was Greg's suggestion to play for clips on the arm. I had seen them play it in this way before but I was properly convinced that this was Greg's fashion of revenge for my loose lips. It was when their games degenerated to this point, and the voices had risen so, that I would roll to my side and put my face into my book. I was contemplating excusing myself when Greg poked his head out of the childish veil of their conversation and asked, soberly, why I had not looked for a place outside of the dormitories.

"I am still on the payroll of the commission, it is free." Or had I continued there to retain my own image as a Panama Man? I believe in some form I feared the solitude. Not for the loneliness, I went to great lengths to achieve a lonely state in that setting. Without their presence my minute successes meant very little. Though I can admit that now, none of that was apparent to me then, and the prospect of where this conversation was going terrified me more than any punch Greg could have thrown. In a game of cards one wields a bit of control.

He took a gnarled stub of a cigar from out of his trouser pocket and stood, gesturing me to follow. The four other men, stuck in their game, did not give notice to the strange exit as we placed ourselves on the steps of the dormitory. This was the first we had been alone in such a protracted manner. On the step below, he made an awkward turn to address me with his eyes and pulled another cigar and offered it to me. I refused with a wave and looked away from him toward the windows of the police station. They were aglow, the policemen waiting to walk the camp and enforce their curfew.

"What is it again that you do in that shed?"

"I polish stones for a jeweller in the city," talking to a cloud of smoke.

"This is your profession, from home?"

"No. I've been trained."

"And you say you are under contract?"

"Yes."

"Gold?"

I could only laugh. Is this why he had treated me so?

"Your skin looks like gold," he said.

"I think it is the hair they judge."

He gave a chuckle and began to talk of his cousin who was soon to arrive from Barbados, exceptional with his hands. Greg asked if my boss was in search of more help.

"It is possible," humouring him.

At this he ground the cigar into the wooden step and we returned to the men. The influence Mr. Kerr spoke of was a mirage.

It was ten in the morning. Like clockwork the man with the tanks on his back and a stack of paper cups left the health building to deliver quinine to the workers. He would walk the Cut at Empire, come back to refill and carry on west to the edges of Culebra. In my first days in Empire, I was required to sip as I had done each day in Culebra. However, with quick intervention from Mr. Kerr I was freed of this, deemed out of harm's way as my work did not call for me to go to the jungle and my shed was bombed with sulphur on the first of each month. So, the quinine man merely waved as he continued to the police station to take with him his escort, for without this the men often refused.

I called over to the creamy-skinned boy who had been standing off by his tree and he trotted his way over and stood at the door to the shed. He had worn holes in both shoes and had peeled back the canvas in boredom. He folded the rubber beneath his foot and played in the dirt with his toes.

I asked if he could read and he stared at me blankly. If I had not used him to deliver stones, I would have questioned his intelligence. But he was smart, or, at the least, clever. I handed him the newspaper and asked him to read a line. He could not. It was what I expected and I was pleased. I was nervous that his curiosity would set him to read my correspondence, benign as it was—*Mr. Kerr, I have gone to Culebra to sell my stones. SB*

I felt the need to account for myself. In truth, I was to visit Robert.

I placed a coin in the boy's hand. "The white man that came to visit this past Sunday," I said. "It is off the Panama train, Avenue K, a grocer is across the street." He nodded and I let go of the paper and he sprung away. Mr. Kerr and his associates had a telegraph for such simple messages. I had an orphaned boy with sorry shoes.

As I approached the storehouse at the edge of Culebra where I would find Robert, I was filled with the same emotion I had when, as an employee at the Virgil estate, I would be asked to arrange the old playroom. Then, I would play in the little chairs that had once held Margaret, Noah and I as we made up our fantasies on rainy days when we were of an appropriate age to be kept in the same company. I would imagine myself back to childhood. The storehouse, which on that day appeared no more than a stone square only slightly larger than my shed with a broken roof covered in boards for the rain, was similarly a monument of my early experience on the Isthmus. Though one that I wished not to recall. The service of Fifty-nine was by no means the first invitation that Robert had extended that I had, in some manner or another, ignored.

It was a building left over from the French, tucked beyond the eastern boundary of the town. Many of the buildings that the Americans had appropriated, especially those outside of Empire, were rather strewn about—houses overlooking aspects of the canal that with the French were only jungle. I doubt the storehouse was used for explosives. I do not believe the main of their attack reached that far, the bone yards with their abandoned machinery were miles away.

A hose from the adjoining water tower had been run through the door and held it open. The cans that had been tied to the door's upper hinge to announce visitors had been removed, maybe thought to be a nuisance, and the door opened without a sound. The counter was littered with the same tacked notes and product specifications it had when I had worked there, only newly layered in parts. Robert, at the back with the hose, did not hear me enter. He hacked at the wooden husk of a barrel with an axe. When a large gape appeared he began to shower it with water from the hose. He was barefoot, as he had always been in his storehouse, though now also shirtless, his trousers rolled up past his calves. The barrel he had disembowelled lay on the ground. He threw the hose aside without closing it, wasting the rainwater that had collected those afternoons. A grey ooze covered the entire stone floor, collecting in thick rivers, and the entire room filled with the nauseating smell of salted wet metal.

When I worked in that shop, Robert would cautiously pick his way around the barrels of explosives. "Trust not a thing," he would say. "It all soon blow." He would not let metal in the shop for fear of a spark. To see him that day with such a fierce disregard, ripping into the wood with an axe, muted me. It was when he began to pry open the top of a small wooden crate that he noticed me.

"Work has kept me busy," I said. It was silly to apologize for my absence, given his feverish activity, but I felt it necessary and so it was the first thing said. He regarded my words with a twisted face and returned to his prying of the crate. "They spit on us," as he lost his balance and fell into the pool of grey that was growing at his feet. He appeared to be sobbing.

I lifted the hinged section of the counter and crossed the room to him. I could feel the trembling muscles of his back. I crouched and offered my hand. The awkward strength of his embrace toppled me and I fell beside him in the pool. He let loose his body and his head fell to my lap. He was laughing.

The floor was cool, the puddle gaining on my linen, a spike of his matted hair tickling my abdomen through my shirt. The heaves slowed and I began to laugh, though I knew not why. He raised himself from my leg to hand me a folded wet square. The paper was stained with powder. I unfolded it carefully but the moist pages ripped easily. It was addressed to Robert Francis Braithwaite, Foreman. It was from the payroll office, but this was all that was legible.

"What does it say?" A bizarre question to ask an illiterate man, I know, but it must have been read to him.

"I will now earn twelve cent and the men ten," he said. "And they have fired two of my men over the service for Fifty-nine."

We had never discussed his finances but this amount, ten cents, was the same as I was paid as a mere runner in my first days on the Isthmus. "Where are the men?"

"I've sent them to Colón to find work."

I stood and lifted him to his feet, walked him to the stool behind the counter. I closed the hose and found hung on a nail his shirt and brought it to him. I told him he must go home to sleep this off and that I would walk with him. I suggested that it may be temporary, went to the corner for the mop while he sat on the stool buttoning his shirt with sopping grey fingers. He argued this point and took the mop from me and dropped it to the floor. Before we left the shed, he gathered some planks of wood and asked that I hold them up as he nailed them to the doorframe. It was a pathetic gesture—the boards were thin and could be ripped with no trouble—but I allowed it.

It was the first time I had been all the way to where Robert had made his home. In my six months running explosives in Culebra, I would walk him to the road and then bid him goodbye as he disappeared into the jungle on the northeast side of Culebra. It was a hundred-metre walk through thick brush. Robert walked this in his bare feet without pause. I was far behind in my boots and tentative advance—eighteen months prior, my eager naiveté would have sent me running through this same jungle with a barrow loaded with explosives.

As we approached, you could hear the bark of a dog. Sensing my nerves, or the fact that I had retreated several steps at the noise, he laughed out, "If

I don't hear that, I pull out my knife." As we got closer, the sound of rolling metal could be heard beneath the menacing noises of the animal. We reached a clearing and there appeared the dog, tied to a stake with a chain. Robert said something to its ear, ruffed it by the neck and let him loose. A brownish mutt with muscled shoulders jumped to me, then began to play this game of gnawing at the back of my boots. The black around his eyes had apparently gifted him with the name Diablo. Though to call this, even with a clap, did nothing to offer a distraction.

Robert toured me through the large hut with a high ceiling and sloping sides that he had fashioned with his own hand out of bamboo, thatched banana leaves and industrial rope when the Americans had begun to make their designs on Panama. He had, in neat order, sacks tied to a support beam that held his dried food and nuts. There were several covered jugs of rainwater spread about the wall opposite the mattress. It was an impressive mattress, a better quality than the canvas bunk in my dormitory. Drinking glasses, plates and utensils were stacked on a miniature bureau to the right of the door. He showed me a prized set of china with the seal of the Canal Commission that he stored wrapped in cotton in an old aluminium icebox. He had won this and his padded mattress in a game of cards with a friend who had janitored the Tivoli Hotel.

I was pointed outside to a large log that had been carved into a flat bench and ran alongside a fire pit. Diablo had tired of his game and exhausted his happiness for his master and sat curled in his self-made groove in the dirt behind the bench. Robert, with a proud smile, appeared from inside the hut with a slice of bun on the china from beneath his bed and placed it on the bench beside me. He disappeared and came again outside with two large jugs of rainwater. He then produced a bar of soap and poured the water over my hands and I lathered them. He took the soap from me and walked around the back and removed his clothes for his standing bath. I do not know what compelled me to observe him, but I was unable to turn away. He threw water to his groin and underarms, then to his entire body, wiping as much of the stink from the storeroom out onto the clay beyond the basin. His muscles were long and stringy, and his breasts sagged to the middle and his belly protruded firmly from herniation. His nakedness flopped as he again threw water to his body and again rubbed the soap. He did this quickly twice more before pouring the leftover clean water over his head and down his backside. He dried his feet and groin with a towel and put on his undershorts and came to join me on the bench.

It was nearing the noonday rains. We set about the task of securing an awning over the log and pit. We did not speak of the storehouse. I did not ask if he intended to return the following morning and face an angry Mr. Strong. Or if he would, at his age, strike off in another direction and find a new job. Or with his surplus retire to the jungle, coming to town only for his canned goods.

"They have given a number to the explosion in the paper. Nineteen. Thirteen silvermen and Fifty-nine is not among the list of dead or injured," I said.

"We need to get you home, to Jamaica," he said. One of his workers was to leave in the coming days.

"I am finally learning more of the trade," I said. "Mr. Kerr has given in. This is why I could not join the service of Fifty-nine."

He smiled.

"When I have learned this, I will go," reminding him that none of us were assured to fetch more than ten cent back home. If he were to give a line about respect, I was prepared to state that respect wouldn't make the world wish to buy Jamaican sugar again. But there was no argument to be had. If I were more aware, this would have been a sign to me.

"You know," he said. "When Kerr first come, it's not you he want."

I disagreed with a shake of my head.

"It's true. I gave to Mr. Strong a tin of Cuban tobacco to choose you. Kerr wanted a St. Lucian or a Spaniard, heard the Jamaican to be lazy."

"So I have the Cubans to thank?"

Oblivious to the direction of his nostalgia, I became caught amongst my own thoughts. I wondered if Robert had invented this sentimentality to give him leverage in his future arguments about my departure. Nonetheless, it was an ego-shattering statement. Had all the pride that I took in my life up to that point turned on the barter of a tin of tobacco? But as I pondered it, it had an opposite meaning. Mr. Kerr took me for a ninny and I had proved him wrong. I had won his confidence.

We waited out the ever-shortening rains on that bench beneath the awning, the muddied drops marking my shoes and Robert's naked feet. As it cleared, he went indoors to change and returned with clean trousers greyed above the knee by the sun. I looked down and saw not his bare feet or his work boots, but a pair of spit-shined black loafers with thinning wooden soles.

"Do you intend to return to the shop? Now?"

He waved my questions away, swinging a shirt over his shoulders and beginning with the cuffs. He looked proud and poor.

"Do you?"

"Let me do this my way, Sam."

"You are a fool!" It was a statement a son might make to a father when he believes he has come of age. "Let things settle. Let your point be made."

He grabbed the tails of his shirt and gave a tug before he slid them into his trousers, smoothed his waistline and looked at me squarely with a tight jaw—a look to suggest that my vision was not yet as clear as I might suspect. Stern as it was, it did not contain an anger.

"We are all fool," he said.

And with this I knew his mind was made. This business of the explosives would set the Commission back no more than an afternoon or two, slight changes might be made in favour of the workers, and the men could have been talked back to work or replaced. But I said no more.

He blindly reached behind him and took from a hook inside the door a belt and began to thread it. It was his intention to end here all along. He, not I, had hustled us from the storehouse so he could carry on with what I had interrupted. He had finally recovered a symbol that he could wield and pour meaning to, and he was not to let go. It is the story of the Isthmus.

Robert left his head uncovered, his hair in its normal knotted mess. He returned to the hut and threw out two bones for Diablo, who only raised his head sleepily to avoid the sprinkling of wet dirt. Robert ruffed his neck again, attached the chain to his collar.

After a slow and silent march, we came to the road. To my right was the way I would walk to Empire and to my left I could see Robert's storehouse in the distance. There had already accumulated a collection of white Zone Police officers moving to the directions of Mr. Strong. He had come, as Robert knew he would, to check the inventory as he did each afternoon. The officers ran in and out of the storehouse, laying the salvageable explosives on a tarp that had been set in the sun.

Robert held me for a moment, his stubble brushing the lobe of my ear as he urged me toward Empire. I took a few steps in this direction and then turned to watch him approach the officers. Mr. Strong saw Robert and came to him, pointed to the storehouse and took off his hat to wipe the sweat that had collected underneath. Robert raised a hand and said something so softly that I could not hear. It was then that Mr. Strong began to shout words distorted by the lump of tobacco imbedded in his cheek. Robert did not appear to flinch as three officers set down their explosives and surrounded him. One applied handcuffs. Another grabbed him by the back of the neck and with the aid of the third tripped him and threw him to the ground. Robert lay with his head pointing away from me. All I could see was the worn wood of his shoes reflecting gold in the sun, a slight twitch. I turned away.

I had done nothing. Add to that, Robert had required that I do nothing. But he was ignorant of the stones that burned in my pocket and to the fact that I found myself on their side. I discarded the stones one by one on the road toward Empire as I walked with my eyes to the dust.

He was given false charges and hung, next to the murderer, on the very same stage we had sat on in the days before. The very same stage that has come to me in my dreams. I was not witness to his execution. When I received news of his extraordinary punishment, despite my progress with Mr. Kerr, I took Robert's advice (telling myself it was what he wanted) and quickly arranged my transport back to Jamaica, convincing myself that I had so narrowly avoided a scar.

I have not seen my spirit in a week and I find myself waking and laughing aloud. As expected, Mrs. Welcome warned me against abandoning her completely and asked that I continue with the regimen until the new year. I will humour her for these few weeks.

Qua has been hurried off by the requests of his mother, loaded with another batch of cakes. For our last lesson I arranged myself more than a metre from him and hung the foul-smelling sheet over the balcony. Though like a nurse caring for a loose-bowelled invalid, none of this appears to bother him.

He seems to enjoy my lessons and for me it is company, his small shining coconut of a head contemplating the simple but immaculately scribed sums that I write on torn scraps of paper. Working with money as he does, the math is really quite easy for him. We are also telling time. My primitive lessons have only been a crude imitation of what I remember from my mother's counting lessons and my first years with Mrs. Hanna. A true shame that he has gone without schooling and will probably only receive what I can offer in exchange for his fleeting company. How we have entered into this unspoken agreement? Does his mother see in my face a lighter and older face of her boy? Does she fear that in time poverty and proving will lead him to another deathly enterprise of the white men? And does she need to believe it will not take such a toll? She does not even know my history, maybe only believes me to be a good-natured coloured gentleman who has fallen on bad luck. What else am I to do but battle myself like this? I had an old deck of cards and in my daylight waking hours would flip them in games of solitaire. But the wear marks soon made themselves obvious and impossible to forget and the game is now quite boring. I have since given them to Qua and I am sure he has yet to mark them as I had, maybe he will imagine a game where this is of no significance. I could have him bring them and we could use them to do figures and sums.

Even with my returning sanity, Mrs. Welcome has focused my thoughts on Panama and it is difficult to turn away. I now remember my departure from Port Antonio. I have somehow kept the vision of Margaret in my head this whole while, though this is the first it has been brought to front. The short cap is pinned to her head, its ribbon blowing in the sea breeze as she stands beside my aunt, waving from the Titchfield Hotel. Did she bring to Georgia that simple pink necklace she had about her neck? There were at least fifty of us that day boarded without contracts and only a slight medical exam—an uncomfortable boney hand on our genitals, a request to cough, a question of venereal disease and our age. And anything could be mended for the price of a shilling.

I reached Colón and stepped down the long, worn and rickety planks, concerned I was to fall into the sea. Two officers began to prod me for papers, papers I did not have. Then came questions in what I believed was Spanish. I only stared blankly and they assumed I was one of the men from Martinique and gave up in their communication, pointing me to the line of workers making their way to the train. I could only watch as the train passed work camps where more assured passengers stepped off. Paralysis brought me from Colón through the entire Isthmus.

I would have stayed riding the train if not for the fear that I would end up back in Colón only to be returned to Jamaica. At nightfall I discovered a tool shed on a farm on the outskirts of the city. All I had brought was useless: my few British coins would not buy me bread in the stores; the two leftover pieces of fried bammy from my aunt had been long devoured; the bottle of kerosene and coconut oil I brought to rub to my skin and do battle with the mosquitoes only flavoured my blood. Luckily, it was February and the rains were months away and the weather was hot and pleasant. The bag I carried about my shoulder I filled with grass. In the morning I rose quickly and with great care so as not to arouse the horse in the neighbouring shed. I spent my first day in the hills looking for fruit. A knife thieved from the shed afforded me the luxury of water and flesh from the coconuts I found cast to the ground. I returned in the evening and hid behind the large grass of the farm, watching the family eat their meats, waiting for the lights in the windows to be extinguished and the beast to stop its restless feet. I had crossed an ocean to make a horse stable my home.

On the second night I cried for my mother and then I cursed her and walked at daybreak the way I had come by train. By noon I had arrived at Culebra and happened upon Robert and his crew cooking river fish, drinking cane liquor and gambling. They had been given the day off out of respect for Washington's birthday. I was then ignorant of this man or his meaning. It is in this introduction that I began with my new surname. They were taken by my skill in dominoes. I shaved small tree branches to a point for Robert, who skewered the fish and watched the fire. It was then I learned to be prudent with that liquor, a cut on my left thumb whose small scar remains is stinging proof.

I asked him if he knew my Uncle Jeffrey from the days of the French. In sloppy gestures I approximated his height and asked him to imagine my face, only darker as my aunt had told me. Of course, he could not recall him but it endeared me to him—this eager high-brown Jamaican, somehow a second-generation Panama Man. The next morning, he took me to meet Mr. Strong. My head ached from the liquor and my only wish was for this man to position his large brimmed hat to block the sun and stop my head from splitting. Robert spoke of my ability to wield a pickaxe. He began to boldly recount a lie of my being a carpenter on an estate in Jamaica. Robert was detailing my duties on the estate (what time I woke to tend to the animals, how I was never once late) when Mr. Strong turned to me, the mountain of his hat eclipsing the sun, "Nigger, you looking for work?" dipping his head to spit. When the blinding glare had cleared, the first man ever to look me square in the eyes and call me a nigger was slowly studying me, and I could not speak. Robert affirmed that this is why we came up here, "To find this hard-working boy a job." I quickly nodded and said, "Yes," so he would not assume I was a dimwit more fit to be an errand boy.

Margaret must be thought a nigger in Georgia, though we have never corresponded on this. My mother's years of work for Mrs. Wolfe and her dressmaking shop to afford Mrs. Hanna and my sister's advanced schooling, wiped away by boat rides, Margaret to the United States and I to Panama. Her son of the mind to be a common digger (just drop the 'd' and add an 'n,' I could imagine her saying—oh, how she would have protested), her daughter on her way to becoming a proper headmistress, but both niggers. What a shock this was to me then.

Within a week of my meeting with Mr. Strong I had finished my apprenticeship with Robert and started to carry the explosives to the men in the Cut. I would rise early so that I may walk alone from my dormitory in Culebra along the ridges of the Cut and then on to Robert's storehouse. I had made a habit of watching the steam shovels aligning to begin their work. The men would crawl silently about these mechanical dinosaurs, lubricating their joints and inspecting their limbs. It seemed a peaceful and rewarding fellowship and I contemplated learning the trade of a mechanic. Because the view into the Cut was of rocks cascading down into a flat valley, it produced an air of permanence. But each day the arrangement of this rock shifted.

The social climate in Culebra was pleasant. Though I spent a good amount of my free hours reading, I was not ridiculed for this. In fact, the men in my dormitory were generally friendly. I assume this was because of the charm of my eagerness and my relationship to Robert. The workers I would pass on the way to my assignments, the West Indians who found themselves in Robert's shop, would address me and I would stop and chat them up about their work. And though it delayed my deliveries, Robert approved of my ambition. It was my intention to graduate from my running duties to that of a full-fledged digger or a member of a drilling gang or a mechanic, as I have said.

On my third day of running explosives, I delivered a full cart to a Spanish crew at the eastern edge. These men, five of them, had dug two holes that a modest amount of powder was to go in. They were to collapse a small ridge and then see how the land fell and continue on with more exaggerated explosions. They were set about the mouth of the second hole, connecting the wires that ran from the first. The men then gestured for me to fetch another box of explosives. As I reached the cart, I heard a gurgling. The DuPont and The Trojan were the primary explosives delivered on the Isthmus. The DuPont was a very effective explosive but gave no warning if it accidentally set its charges. The Trojan, which was used that day, would turn a pinkish colour and get to boiling when it was to ignite. And so I grabbed the closest man by the arm and started to run and yelled for the others to follow. Then came the showering. The wires had already been hooked, so the explosives in both holes and everything from the nearby cart detonated.

One of the men, confused or slow-footed, had not run with us. We returned for him when the debris had settled and found him trapped under a large boulder. The Spanish were frantic in the language that I had yet to even grasp. They pointed to me and all of us crouched to one side and rolled the boulder. We did this carefully as we were on unsteady ground and in danger of ourselves falling down the ridge. Anything resembling breath had been crushed in this man. His skull stuck to the rock as it was lifted. When it came loose it fell to the rock below as would a wet newspaper. One man went to arrange to have the body carried away properly. The others walked a distance in separate directions. I stood, disbelieving.

A piece of stone had punctured my cheek just above my jaw and left a triangle scar that remains beneath my thick beard. I was sent to the local infirmary to be stitched, returned later to my dormitory to find the Spanish crew waiting at the door. I was too naïve, only days in, to know that this was not a normal sight—goldmen at the door of a coloured dormitory. They had gone to fetch the money train and the boss had received my first payment on the Isthmus for me. The three men threw in a portion of their own. This is the first of the money that would eventually transport Margaret to Georgia. I have still kept the receipt for this transfer, worn and long faded now, as a marker between the pages of my reading books. After they had given their money, they shared words and then quickly excused themselves to return to their side, giving thanks once more in their own language. There was no talk of their dead crewmember. This silence in regard to the dead, I would find, was quite common.

It would be six months before I was rescued from the work of running explosives through the Cut by Mr. Kerr and placed in my shed in Empire. In that time there was not a word shared between Robert and myself of this accident, though given his position I am certain he was aware. He never once pointed to my cheek and asked for a story.

It was the only time on the Isthmus that I witnessed a death. I had counted the bodies on the trains as they passed tarped (dead from malaria and other unfortunate explosions), but this is not a similar thing. And with this singularity came a resonance, the impossibility of forming a callus. Not a moment of my time in Culebra was immune to the imaginings of this poor man's death—either by the blasting of stone or by the weight of that same stone. The picture of this depleted chest and skull has lived within me all this while.

If Margaret had her way, I would not have gone to Panama. And we might have come upon other means to finance her degree and passage to the United States. I could have stayed, left my pitiful job with Mrs. Virgil and found work as a bookkeeper, saved my money slowly. Maybe even found a way to go to Georgia with her. But Panama seemed the clear path.

The daylight has left and the lampmen have arrived. If I am fortunate, I will sleep straight through—I will soon break myself of this ridiculous schedule I have accustomed myself to. Tomorrow Qua and I do not have our lessons, his mother is again sending him to all corners of the city with her cakes for the holidays. I am actually looking forward to this break in our tutoring. If I do sleep well, I will treat myself and pay the two pence to take the Belt Line all the way through Cross Roads and back.

Near dusk, a few hours after I have returned from a difficult climb up the stairs to my flat. It has taken me this long to simply recover, inhaling a rag soaked with the peppermint liniment Mrs. Welcome had given me for my wrist.

I threw my coins in the flat pan the conductors now wear slung about their shoulders and sat with my back to him so my view was not to be disturbed. The twists down Darling Street onto Barry then to West were the worst of the trip, but was I ever rewarded. This was my first view of the harbour south of the Parade in almost half a year. I sat in the shade of the covered car but the sun was heavy on the water, an island of light splitting the deep blue. I took a sip from the flask in my breast pocket as we made our way toward East Street and up to Cross Roads and rested my legs on the empty chair beside me, turning to face the conductor and the harbour as we travelled inland. I am now even looking south down Princess Street, through the tenements with the aluminium roofs, visualizing the majesty of the water.

When I disembarked and made my way the short distance toward my flat, the winds were alive and breathing as they do here in December. All the women and children were out with their gossamer veils drawn over their faces. I was left with picking the lapel of my worn jacket up to my mouth. Feeling my breath coming short, I walked a half block out of my way, figuring that I might see Qua playing races with his friends down Princess Street as I often spy from my balcony before he reports to his mother for more orders. They float pieces of wood in the running water of the gutter and wager their farthings. But he was not there, the gutters dry and the wind howling with unbearable dust in that tight alley. All that is to be said is that I opened the door almost on my knees and breathed through the rag until my senses were renewed.

A group of four boys have trapped a rat in a rum crate and sit lazily in a line on the sidewalk, the boys Qua's mother detests. They wait until the rat noses its way to the lip of the crate to examine an escape to throw their stones. The sharp squeal can be heard from my balcony. I imagine the quiet and confused retreat of small meaty feet. One boy takes a bottle of liquor from his waist and pours it in every corner of the crate. It appears they are to light this animal on fire.

I raise myself with my elbows and yell for their attention, but it seems I have only accelerated their pace and made their game more enjoyable. Another boy strikes a match while the others implore him to do it quickly. If the animal has made a noise, it cannot be heard above their ravings. The flames die down and the animal, I presume, is dead. It seems they have the same curiosity. One has gone up the street to retrieve a stick and now prods at the charred insides of the crate. They have already begun to retell the experience, to build the extraordinary exaggerations for the days to come. I soothe myself with the thought that at least Qua is not among them.

Someone whose tone they respect has called for them. They drag the blackened crate off the road with the stick and into the crevice of a building. It is only now that something resembling the smell of the dead animal carries to my balcony. It is of hair and skin and bones, of blood.

The lampmen have come and gone, and come and gone again, and I do not recall their faces or their footsteps. I spent this past night crying, a wash of things forgotten. I have lived these last nine years walking on a lake softly frozen in March, staying to the tiniest of edges.

After I leave Robert on the road being carried away, I return to my dorm. I write in bed, disorganized thoughts until I fall into a sleep with my journal and pencil on my chest. There comes a hard knock and two men in the doorframe wearing the short-billed hat of the police. My first thought is that a man in another dormitory complained of noise, but it had been a tame night for the men and as I wipe the stick from my eyes I see it is the lightening dark of early morning.

"Who is Sam Brown?" the taller officer asks as he ducks his head to avoid the centre beam. The other men, beginning to rise in angry curses, unwind when it was my name that is called.

I raise my hand, thinking perhaps they have been sent to deliver an urgent message from Mr. Kerr. The second officer carries a lantern and walks about the room as the taller one approaches my bed. His skin is both black and grey, a charcoaled black. I vaguely remember a thick beard just at the chin.

"You're Brown?"

I think of Robert and the afternoon, sit facing him and reach to the shelf above my bed for my papers. I am in my singlet and undershorts, my feet square on the grimy wooden slats.

He examines my papers.

"Hands," he says.

I look at him in confusion.

"In front."

He gives no reasons while Greg and the others tuck themselves deeper in their sheets. I continue to ask what I have done and he only continues to demand my hands. "Out front," he says. I take them from my lap to my knees. His partner interprets this belligerence. "Like this," setting down the lantern and sticking his palms together and drawing in his elbows. He then continues to walk in figure eights about the bunks. If this was not a serious matter, they would prod the other men and demand their papers. They have come for me. The one who carries the light unties a rope that has been dangling from a belt loop and hands it to the other. These black officers have been given a club and a rope and have run with this authority.

"Where are you to take me?"

Still nothing.

"At least let me dress."

He pauses in his rope tying, reverses the few tight circles he has made. Searching my bunk he discovers the paper sack with my ruined nightclothes. He opens it and the foul smell of excrement escapes. Amused, he throws the sack to my lap, pulls the club from his hip and waits for me to change as he flips through my journal.

When I am done he remains at a small distance staring at my disgrace. Then he begins again with the rope. By the time he reaches my elbows I cannot feel my fingertips. He takes the St. Lucian's hat and puts it to my head, the two laughing at the outfit they have assembled as I am led barefoot out the door. I look over my shoulder at the collection of belongings that are being left behind (a razor, soap, books). They may wait a day but, if I do not soon return, they will begin playing for these and that will conclude their memory of me.

The waiting train is aimed at Culebra. What have I done that is deserving of such a demeaning shackle? My thoughts stray and I take an errant step. My tall policeman gathers the slack rope around his fist and gives a hard pull. My arms attempt to leave their sockets and I fall. I am thrown up with hands in my armpits. My ridiculous top hat tumbles. Before it is replaced, the shorter policeman cleans it as a porter would for a distinguished white guest. This is intended to be a spectacle, but there is no one about the camp this early before dawn, though the men of my dormitory have no doubt gathered by the one window and are squinting through its dusty pane.

The train is stopped at the western border of the camp, adjacent to the Central Division Administration Building. The white conductor sees the odd collection of blacks approaching and bolts from the car to argue with my escorts. The shorter policeman places his hand at my shoulder, an instruction to move no further, and the tall policeman has taken the lead rope to its maximum. The confrontation escalates and my arms began to move with his. It is clear—we will not ride in the cab of his car. The policeman reminds the driver that he is one of the few black goldmen, and of a higher rank. The conductor spits and I am jerked forward.

It is a compromise. The shorter, holder of the lamp, will ride on the footrest beyond the cab. My policeman has thrown me in first to buffer the space between himself and the white man. To this conductor I am no more than a log that has been strapped to one of his cars and called for in Culebra. I stare at the coming tracks and the passing mule-driven cart traffic heading between Culebra and Empire. Thirty minutes by foot, half that by mule, this man pulls his cargo in what must have been less than five minutes.

Mr. Kerr is standing by the depot, unsmiling and pacing. There had been no such thing, a depot on this grand a scale, when I had lived and worked here, the short season Robert had talked about. The Americans toss the word progress around and this is how they justify it—there is no station for niggers to dry their rain-soaked clothes, but we have built a proper depot at Culebra.

"You were ordered to escort him!"

The two that were so bold with the driver of the cab bow their heads and mutter apologies. Mr. Kerr dismisses them with promises that he will alert their superiors and immediately unties the rope from my arms and wrists.

"Have they hurt you?"

I shake my head. It is neither yes nor no. I want him to massage my hands but do not ask. There is a large spec of dirt at the corner of my eye and I wipe at it with an awkward arm.

"The Warden wishes to speak with you. It's best he say." There is little softness in his voice.

"And I with him." I say this with a rush of confidence and then look to my pants.

"I will see about fetching you some clothes. And be cautious with him."

It is rising time in Culebra and, now, I am a spectacle, walking in my soiled and stinking nightclothes, fine hat and bare feet. We walk through a garden, past the Governor's House to a large structure with two long hallways stretching from a guarded entranceway. It is raised by steps for the rain, its only remarkable aspect. It is wood, painted the same chalky white as the rest of the administration buildings.

We enter through the left flank and Mr. Kerr pauses to wipe the dust from his feet on a mat that lies by the door. I begin to do the same and am reminded that I am without shoes. A sunburnt guard regards Mr. Kerr with a smile and opens the door. We pass an empty, large holding cell. Only the echoes of his shoes are heard. It is the kind of building, with high ceilings and thick walls, that evokes a nervous quiet. Mr. Kerr has sped ahead or I have slowed. He waits at the end of the hall holding an open door as I walk past the adjoining cell.

A man sleeps curled in the corner. The cell stretches back a distance and the light is bad. Another man sits on the edge of an upturned crate close to the gate of the cell. A freshly swollen and bloodied face looks up at me. It is Robert. He squints to recognize me and I am unable to look away. His right eye is swollen shut, but his left knows me. I pull the iron gate to my cheeks. He wears the same buttoned shirt, bloody and ripped at the shoulder. He looks to my feet, pale and pinkish, and his beaten face contorts. There is blood leaking through his pant and onto the crate. He can make no effort to stand.

Mr. Kerr gives an empty cough and I push myself away. Is this why they have roped me like a goat and brought me here? Because I have held a pitiful plank of wood as my friend nailed it.

"They are the worst of the lot," Mr. Kerr says when I reach him. I do not understand his meaning. He leads me to a sitting room adjacent to the office of the Warden. It is small and cluttered with well-appointed things. A broad shouldered assistant dressed in military regalia raps on the Warden's door, opens it and instructs us with a finger to the two seats at the corner of the desk. Mr. Kerr urges me along with a nod.

The chairs are wooden and have the same seal that has been marked on the Warden's door and on Robert's china. The assistant's work is done and he returns to the hallway. To create a more acceptable appearance, I place my hat on top of my bare feet. My eyes shift over the framed pictures of men in uniform and the tightly stuffed brown leather throne where the Warden will soon sit. It is lined with a golden thread, and his table, an oak slab as thick as my arm, is bigger than my cot in the dormitory. I had heard stories of the ships that came to dock at Colón and brought luxuries to entertain the American officials, but not here in the heart of the place where nature had made her point.

Mr. Kerr has said not a word and purses his lips in such a manner that I am to understand that we will not talk. It is clear that he is not the summoner. He has been summoned as well.

"No! No! No!"

A commotion from the sitting room just beyond the closed door. I can hear low and urgent voices. Footsteps and a door is shut. Nothing else until the Warden appears with a sudden crash. He rolls along on his cane looking just as surprised as me at the accompaniments of his own office. A leashed Shepherd follows him, brushes by my seat and pauses to smell me. Mr. Kerr stands and I follow suit, hoping the dog will move away, but he continues to nuzzle about my thigh. The Warden takes a moment to catch his balance and, when he realises his animal has not followed the routine, taps his cane and points it to the corner.

"On your spot!" and the dog obliges. The Warden throws his cap to the desk and hobbles to his seat. "Good day, boy, good day." Is this my greeting? Or is he again talking to the dog? I remain standing with my knees bent, hiding as much of my nightclothes below his desk as is possible. He settles in his chair and, like a clock's hands that have just struck their hour, stops his twitch on me. I sit.

"Can you read, boy? 'Course you can, Mr. Kerr likes his boys literate."

I do not answer for I believe he does not wish for me to.

"Have you been reading the papers?" He throws a folded *Star and Herald* across the ocean of his desk. At this gesture the dog inches from his spot. He slaps a flat palm on the dog's head and stares at me as if none of this has happened and so I turn my face to the paper. It is the paper that has announced the execution of the murderer. I had read it several times but give it a serious look. I will wait for him to tell me what this is about. The Warden, sweating at the task of containing his seemingly erupting insides, speaks English as I do, but as I have often experienced on the Isthmus, I am at a loss of fluency.

It is seven in the morning, if that, and abandoned, liquor-tinted cubes of ice are already melting in the bottom of one of the empty glasses. I have been dragged from my bed and forced to wear shit-stained clothes and this man, incapable of physical labour on the canal, has a mechanism to produce ice for his morning brandy. He makes his way to the window where far away the steam shovels of The Cut can be seen starting to move their monstrous limbs.

"Mr. Kerr says that you'll be a help." He says this without turning in my direction. "There is another man we will hang alongside the murderer."

"Sir." My lips are sticky with silence. I clear my throat to be heard. "What has the other done? This paper speaks of one man." Unless he is hiding something, he is unaware that I am connected to Robert.

"This one has been subversive."

I hear the paces of the assistant's wooden shoes in the hall.

"But what has *this one* done that warrants death?"

"He has destroyed property and organized a worker's rebellion." Mr. Kerr says this in a lower voice.

The Warden turns from his position, his near-bald head wet with sweat, and looks toward Mr. Kerr and then to me. "Our evidence also suggests that he is responsible for the death of another canal worker."

It is easily read as a lie, but this is of little issue. "And it has not made the paper?" I ask with blatant sarcasm. I stare at the peculiar tuft of hair at the right of his head I had first noticed when he made his visit to Mr. Kerr's shop.

"Has Mr. Kerr explained to you that you will be rewarded?" His back is again to me, leaning on a bureau of the same dark oak.

"I have been carried from my bed to this room without a word." I study Mr. Kerr. If I am a dog in this world, then he is only a child. "I will have no part in this," I say. It is an honest statement. I collect my hat and begin to stand.

"You are not free to go," loud enough for the assistant posted by the door to hear and in a tone he will understand. The broad-shouldered man enters the room, shuts the door and clasps his hands behind his waist. They are practised at this and merely wait for my decision.

"And why am I not free to go?"

"Mr. Kerr has informed me that you have stolen from a grocer in the city. That is a very serious offense."

Mr. Kerr looks away.

"I will make my statement, my word to his."

"Your crime carries an indefinite term left to my discretion. Do you intend to test that?"

"This is not justice." First you humiliate me then you threaten me is the line that comes to me, but I have used up all of the belligerence to which I am entitled. The assistant has stepped forward and there is no need for him to do more. I sit and ask the Warden to make him leave.

When the door has been closed and his pacing begins again, I speak.

"And the other man. What is to happen to him?"

"That is a separate issue. He will be hung, regardless."

The Warden has created a statement, one that I am to sign. He pushes a copy of the document across the desk. "The original is at the Governor's House," he says. I do not read it. It is to make this other charge stick, I know. They soften their tone. Mr. Kerr adds that I have been chosen because I have been such an outstanding worker and Isthmian citizen. I do not look in his direction. I inquire of the reward. They stumble their words. I make my demands: I wish to leave safely to Kingston; I wish to be given a sum and a modest retirement. It means little to them—or less than this man dead. (I find myself starting to refer to Robert in a nameless way, even to myself.) It is also, I feel, all I can ask for in the circumstance. Some eminence in the United States is turning the screw to the high officials on the Isthmus, who in turn have pressured the Warden, to Mr. Kerr, to his Brown, &c. I am aware of my place. I want my terms in writing and signed, though I know it means nothing. The Warden makes another sign for his assistant, who in turn fetches a secretary who runs in with a typewriter in arms.

"And what will be recorded in the paper?"

He appears baffled by my concern. The dog has snaked from his spot and is sniffing at my feet from beneath the table.

"There will be a line on his crimes and an announcement for the execution."

The Warden rises from his desk and walks again to the window. Mr. Kerr's eyes are on me. I ask to be left for a minute. It is the last gift of my leverage.

Robert is just metres away, behind three closed doors, one long hallway and an iron gate. It is now, hours before I am to leave the Isthmus, that I begin to understand the Americans' obsession with compartments. The sitting room leads to another hallway where a man is reading telegrams regarding the American officers that are soon to arrive, their breakfast allergies. In another cubicle a secretary is passing a note, with a giggle, to a general's visiting son whom she thinks to be handsome. I take off my nightclothes, ball them and throw them to the Warden's gold-plated dustbin. I am sitting in the Warden's chair in my underclothes wiping at my face with my wrists when Mr. Kerr raps on the door. Without words he disappears. Twenty minutes later he returns with a grey suit and a starched shirt. And a pair of shoes. The suit and shirt are properly hung and near to the right size, no doubt from one of the officers whose duties force him to sleep in his office. The spongy leather of the soles of the shoes are warm with a moist sweat. Nearly a well-dressed man, we begin to walk the way we had come an hour before. I pull at his arm before we reach the hallway.

"Take me another way."

We exit via the cubicles and all do their best to look away. And I am in no mood to look for shoeless men. At the Governor's House I say very little. A man in a heavily adorned military uniform shakes my hand. A good man by my judgement, if that can be trusted, who is seemingly unaware of all that passes before him, for even their justice is cubicled. To his questions I answer yes and make my mark on the statement the Warden has prepared. Mr. Kerr carries me to Colón to board the liner, stuffs a pile of bills in my suit and hands over my leather satchel and instructs me how I am to recover my ill-gotten retirement. All this before the noonday rains.

He came to me in my sleep. Not hanging, not at first, merely paraded on the stage, hands tied and head hooded in a vegetable sack. Because it is never enough to hang a man, the executioner would step away and those around me would throw stones the size of grapefruits. Then he was led to the crate below the crossbeam. I will not reconcile that this is Robert who has brought the jungles of the Isthmus to my balcony. And it is not forgiveness I ask, just for this payment to be finished. Why not haunt the makers of the great canal who sent thousands of us like lame dogs rooting through a maze of rock and mud? One dog limps home to be stuck in a cage and the quarrel is with me? If I would have strung Robert from the gallows myself and waited till he turned from man to corpse, would I, too, have roads and schools in my honour? I once read a paper that rumoured of their chief officers finding a new home in an asylum in some remote part of their country. What I would do to be locked far away, wheeled to the sun and a lovely lawn, fed medicine on the hour.

Qua returned from Mrs. Welcome with a jar of reddish syrup and the instruction to pour this on a potted bush and place it at the edge of my balcony. I was to wait for what he called the god-bird. If it came, I was to believe all is well. Through his demonstrations I knew him to be speaking of the humming bird. It was a halfpenny in his palm and he turned out the door as if none of this, this education, were abnormal. I rose from my afternoon rest with a bloody and cracked body on the floor beside me, brilliant red feathers dulled by hours of death.

I shovelled all of my pennies to sway Qua from his mother's work to be my company all the way to Mrs. Welcome's for his second visit of the day, though only for him to stand outside throwing pebbles in protest. I forced him to revert to simple childish pleasures, robbed him of the sorcery that he has found to take place within. But I did not want to be alone. Even she is at a loss. A god-bird had been killed (or somehow killed itself in such a contorted manner) and had been thrown to me and of this she wanted no part. In nearly every Sunday edition there is news of an obeah being accused of extortion, but to the woman I have given my faith my money is no longer good. Abandon was the word floating behind her glistening tongue. "This is beyond my power," is all she said. Not a syllable rushed. Upon leaving I realised I was given my last suggestion.

I have put on my Sunday clothes and now sit under the cotton tree at the Parade where I am to bury the bird. Shrouded in a now bloody handkerchief and placed in a jewellery box, I choose to believe it at peace. For my tools I have only a chisel of Britannia silver, one of the spoils I purchased upon my return from Panama. I sit on a leg of this cotton tree, resting my back on its back. There are at least twenty tentacles making humps about the ocean of dirt and grass. Only those churchgoers crossing the square take notice of me, and of those I doubt any have the imagination to understand the silver between my legs. They most likely make me a man who has just left the same service they have dallied from. I look at the plot I have finished, a patch of brown in the green the rains have sprung, and cannot help but chuckle. In Panama I would deliver explosives designed to do away with a shelf of dirt much larger than the size of this entire square.

Staring at the Ward Theatre, it strikes me that my sister was long gone to Georgia before the earthquake and before this pale blue giant was erected on the exact spot as the Municipal Royal of our youth. I was present at the inaugural show. Then, on my walks down to the harbour to display my wares, and again on my return, I would pass the theatre surrounded by scaffolding and watch the workers. It was December when the doors opened to anyone willing to pay two shillings to sit in the gallery to see an amateur company perform *The Pirates of Penzance*. Half my month's rent and I did not hesitate to do so, to stand among a crowd that only my skin and my crooked pension deserved me. The production was said to have had "costumes identical to the Savoy," though of course I will never know. I must say that in that time of free living I accepted my mother's wish for me to take advantage of my shade and run toward an easier life. But that evening I was as buffoon as Gilbert's Modern Major General, my clothes reeking of a feathered top hat, and I surely appeared to ride a mule to my seat in the gallery.

Beyond Robert, these past years I have largely avoided thinking around this idea of ancestry. Pinned to my wall next to Margaret's most recent class picture is the one of our mother. I know her dark eyes, they are mine. But it seems it is true that no one ever really knows his own begetting. My grandfather, who I know nothing of other than he farmed cane and shares my same large nose, dies. Soon after, my uncle ventures to Panama for the first attempt at the

74

canal, to earn money for the family. He too finds death, with the French. My mother, as a young girl, wishes to follow the trend of the time and flee the toil of the country for the new capital and an education. My aunt is sent to watch over her and takes work as a mid-wife and steward for the Virgils while my mother does minor housework. City life is harder than my mother expects and she is forced to abandon her studies and learn the trade of a seamstress, working for Mrs. Wolfe until this woman takes ill. I was born more than a year after, my sister three. This much can be figured. And that my father is some white man. All else is possibility.

I have dozed and now he rests before me, hanging. The sky is dark, the square is empty and the light in the Police Corner has been closed. Have I been taken for a man without a home and pitied, not bothered this close to Christmas? This flesh for the first time before my waking eyes. In near forty minutes he has not moved. Is this what had frightened me to soaking my body in garlic and taking my rest only in the daylight? He hangs. How else can one describe a hanging man? His breath, which is still intermittently alive, also hangs in a moment of calm before it is let go. Even the blood of his cheek. All he can do is drip and heave, and sway, I imagine, if there were a wind to come play with him.

Yet, with this spoonful of dirt covering the carcass of a dead bird and a hanging man above my head, my thoughts wander to Qua. This morning I am to tutor him. It feels like a lifetime since he last sat on my floor. I have unravelled and put myself back together in that span, though I cannot say I am prepared to face him—a loose ball of collected string. He has been taught lessons in wizardry, where is the magic in my simple numbers and letters? Maybe he can join me in the night and I can teach him what I know of the stars.

The moon is not in the sky. It has been hiding closer and closer to dawn and will soon disappear. The Hunter I do see to the east as he is from my balcony. I will tell Qua he is hunting the moon and those stars are the rocks he hurls, for his club is now out of distance. *The moon, you see, a tease, for it bides its time in the shadow of the earth only to creep upon the Hunter yet again, tap his shoulder and then catapult past him once more. The Hunter is far from agile and never thinks to turn and meet this foe that moves like clockwork through the patterns of his strewn rocks. He stays his vigil, stick raised to clobber, but is always surprised. The moon is far too cunning to be killed with mere sticks and stones, but the Hunter does not learn this, will not lower his stick and listen for the moon's path. Though maybe in each sky it is not the same Hunter, the offspring bound by the ignorance and arrogance of their fathers, their kind doomed to be dunce and die hungry.*

But Qua's mother will never allow him to venture out past dark, even if it were to join his benevolent benefactor for a lesson on the cosmos. My thoughts at least now loose, though I still have no plan for the boy. I can only stare at the bloodletting hunter that has strung himself and simply waits. The fog runs through King Street from the harbour and is to own this square in a matter of moments. I should set about packing my satchel before I am left to find my way blindly between faintly glowing posts. He remains, and will remain, I suppose. How much breath is there to be in one hanging man?

Crackerasssuckafool

It started with a fall.

Well, that is not entirely true. If there are such things as beginnings, something he toyed with in his academic work, it started, this time, in the Kroger parking lot after he picked up his infant son from daycare with elastic boogers and a 102° fever.

It was not so much that she thought he was stealing his own baby, it was her impulse to announce this to him. Even more because by that point he sensed that it was no longer an accusation in her mind. Nor was it an apology.

It was after the smiling head nod he involuntarily gave all in his new hometown that he spotted a stray cart between two cars and abruptly turned toward it. Why carry the car seat the long walk when he could roll it? Besides, his son loved to look up at him and feel the rattle from the concrete.

When he darted to the cart he saw in his periphery that his movement visibly shook this woman. Recovered, as they were now nearly side-by-side, she turned to him: "I was suspicious you were stealing that baby," she said. "That you were going to put him in another car." A slight laugh.

He mirrored this laugh and followed her the awkward three hundred some feet to the automatic doors. And honestly, by the time he picked up the Motrin and some hummus for his wife, the exchange had left his mind. Sadly, he was accustomed to such encounters in his life, even in the larger, more liberal cities he had lived in. However infrequent, they were frequent enough.

It was on his return to the car, after singing to distract the boy as he leaned in to wipe snot, that it dawned on him. Light skinned as his son was, favoring his mother, *this woman thought I was carrying someone's white baby… and this ignited for her some inborn obligation.*

He grew furious at his own laugh, muted and uncomfortable as it had been.

His planning was immaculate. The New Faculty Welcome was set for the following Monday. As all large events did, it was to take place in the school's in-name-only chapel. His new colleagues and the entire administration would be in forced attendance as he and others were paraded across the stage. When his name was called, before kind words could be said of him, his left shoulder shook. Then a wobble, his knees knocking—some among them may have begun the thought that he was dancing. But he tripped and sent himself careening into the marble sarcophagus of the fallen Confederate general ominously placed in the chapel's apse. The crowd gasped as it rose in unison.

He was careful not to bang his head, but stayed on the floor with a bedazed look as if he had. Those on stage rushed to him. The dean of the college waved them away so that he could have air while a woman he recognized from the president's inauguration searched the spot where he had tripped, perhaps making sure the university would be free of liability.

Three days later he came with his doctored note diagnosing his adult-onset Tourette's, feigning tears in the Office of Employee Relations while requesting an accommodation. He told the woman across the desk that he had been warned that authority and crowds may cause symptoms to arise and, though things may progress, this particular doctor foresaw nothing that would impede his path toward tenure.

He watched videos online, practiced with his wife and in front of the mirror, and was sure to pepper in smaller yet noticeable episodes as he sat in various department meetings and events related to diversity that he had been volunteered for.

That was it as fall turned to winter and winter to spring.

Midway through his family's summer vacation in Panama he sent the meticulously constructed email to that same woman behind the desk, informing her that his syndrome had, unfortunately, progressed to include a vocal tic. To gear up for the coming term, his regimen now included grocery stores and buses as his family toured the nation of his father's birth. He knew even if his English was understood, the context would most likely not be. And his son was not yet two and so would not remember these days in his life—though he and his wife giggled in bed one morning at the prospect of infecting their child's first words.

Almost a year to the day from his ambush of the general, the university planned an event, a lightly attended open forum to discuss the tepid implementation of only a portion of the recommendations from the Committee on Race and Institutionally Necessary Growth and Engagement. Depending on whom you asked, this was either an earnest undertaking or a cover-your-ass reflex to the events in a nearby town the year prior. The gathering was to be attended by, among others, the university president and some assigned-to-be-concerned members of the board of trustees, and was designed as a serious-faced celebration of the university's long and arduous journey coming to grips with its somehow suddenly recognizable history.

The Q&A segment arrived, as did a congratulatory reaffirmation of the "self-evident" mission of the university. Those on the dais and the small crowd appeared anxious to make their way to the stand of craft beer and macaroons. He waited until the president returned to the podium to declare a successful adjournment before he stood. The question he asked of the president was, from his perspective, rather innocuous and sought to understand how the powers that be felt the forthcoming actions would impact the retention of black students and faculty, a stated need of the institution. Trapped in his tone was the fact that he thought their efforts would not.

The president turned to those seated to his left, and after an interminable moment, broken only by the ungraceful adjusting of one chair, he was still met by only silence.

"Well, in my experience, compromise," the president started. Before he could continue, the tic announced itself for the first time. Twice, in fact. As if shot from a gun.

This time there was no gasp, and no rising from those surrounding him. They did look to the stage, many having expressed genuine if clumsy condolences in the months prior—one sharing the story of a distant cousin "similarly touched." He did not flinch, or laugh, as he fruitlessly awaited an answer to his question. In the stillness, his mind carried back to an afternoon, years earlier, when he was a university student sitting on the stoop of his girlfriend's apartment. He had more hair then that he let go wild and was wearing the quite-expensive-though-baggy purple Karl Kani jeans his mother bought him over winter break. Two elderly women intent on doing good approached him and offered a boxed meal that he rejected, again too kindly, and again laughing reflexively. They walked away, possibly embarrassed, to take their Meals on Wheels elsewhere. Then, he buried the interaction and went about his life. Today, he felt a release and a vague diminishing of an inside thing.

The next morning, at the urinal, the provost, who ritualistically peered over the partition to ask of his day after smiling with big teeth, neither confirming nor denying the existence of an actual bond, did so again.

This was the last time he was somewhat in control.

Elegy for the Sweet Tempered

I hadn't yet met Sascha. I was in Rabat with another girl and we were lost in the markets. A man helped and we followed him to a house full of art and dried fish. It surfaced just this morning, sitting in the rental in front of the bakery, waiting for the college kid to pull the sandwich board to the curb and open the doors, that the man wrapped the fish in frayed white cloth before he pointed us toward our rented flat. And that on the walk, like tourists, we bought too many dates. And that I was on the terrace waiting for a playoff score to update on my phone while the girl was in the kitchen organizing the plate for us to share. He had a gun and he knew where she lived, the woman who had sublet my apartment had written. He took her to the alley. This was nearly all she wrote. And that she was sorry to have told me this and a friend had gathered her. And that my apartment would be empty until I returned.

I'm back at the hotel with all of this and Sascha is still asleep, her shirt stained at the breast and not even an ounce of pumped milk in a bottle on the bedside table. I date the milk and take it to the fridge with the rest. It's the stick of the door that wakes her. She's on an elbow massaging her scalp and ready to nurse, but Darius isn't here. I smile and hand her one of the cookies.

"Go fuck yourself and your cookies," spilling out a laugh.

We are just beginning to laugh.

"I want coffee," she says from the closet as she holds her green-and-white polka dot dress against her hips.

"Let's just get the cookies over with."

It was her idea to go back to the NICU. I convinced her to let Darius sleep at my mom's. We traveled all this way and it'd be cruel not to carve out some time, no matter how "heavy a presence," Sascha's mantra, my mom is. When Darius was born, Sascha announced that family wouldn't be able to visit until we left the hospital. He was jaundiced and we were told it would be a day or two. We stayed nine and my mom came anyway, and Sascha knew we couldn't complain—the baby in the neighboring bed was taken for brain surgery on our second day and hadn't returned by the time we left. When we were on the plane back to LA yesterday, she thought the cookies would be nice. I doubted they'd remember us.

As we cross the street, Sascha takes the bakery box from me. Eight months ago, after the nine days, leaving the hospital wasn't the exit I'd imagined. I crossed the parking lot in the dark, stood in the elevator that had reeked of piss since we arrived, and in thirty minutes the three of us were home. Today there is sun and we walk through the front door and the gift shop is open.

When the buzzer sounds and the NICU doors click, three mothers are being led to the room where infant torsos the dull color of airplane window shades wait for them. "Take a seat and get familiar," Sascha whispers, attempting a version of the CPR trainer we know will enter shortly. Each time we'd seen this parade we rattled on about how absurd it all was. And it was and is. Six or seven others who haven't slept more than two hours at a stretch in at least a week will be in this room. While our crew was refreshingly democratized by this circumstance and this exhaustion—lululemon meeting three-inch, sparkling acrylic nails meeting whatever we were to them—if they wanted any of us to learn how to save a choking baby, that wasn't the time for the demonstration.

A nurse comes at us with open arms before we can even announce ourselves and I'm surprised to recognize her. With my clumsy hug and the smell of Ivory on her bicep comes the memory of how brown Darius was under the bili lights. She's the only nurse on the floor that was with us, but she feels the need to introduce the others on this shift. Somehow, months and countless babies later, she has kind things to say about us. Sascha shows pictures of Darius from Christmas. Another nurse, wearing all manner of unicorn from head to toe, asks for one. "If it's OK," our nurse interrupts. "We can put it on the screen in the waiting room. It gives the parents hope."

I excuse myself, knowing Sascha will start taking pictures with the staff. On the toilet without the need to shit, I find an email from three months after the woman who sublet my apartment was raped. I had followed up and she had moved back to New York. In the exchange, unprompted, I had apparently apologized for the neighborhood. I remember wanting to say more, how I felt guilty, but having some sense not to. Her return email was sweet and silent.

I'm searching the Internet for variations of her name when a man comes into the stall next to mine. I flush, wash my hands and hustle out just as he begins to grunt what I'm convinced are the drums from that Queen song.

Sascha is waiting by the elevators.

"*You,*" she says.

I ask if she's hungry.

"What do you think?"

88

We park down the block from our first apartment and head to the diner with the manhole blueberry pancakes across from the park, only to find it's been turned into a tattoo parlor. *The Sloth & The Bee.* Five years since we moved even further east in the city, before leaving altogether for my job, and with the distance these names are that much more obnoxious. Living the past months in a small southern college town with no billboards and pretty much just an IHOP and a Waffle House for breakfast doesn't help.

"Your people," I say. "Next they'll open *Billie's Groat* and only serve oat milk lattes."

She impersonates a laugh, affirming some sort of solidarity and rhythm. But if I'm honest, the neighborhood was this way when we were here. And that's part of why we came. She lets me pull her close by the crepe belt of her dress and I suggest we walk to the deli we'd passed on the drive over. It's still in the thirties back home and who knows when the weather will turn.

"Should only be ten minutes," I say.

My guess is that it's nostalgia that draws Sascha to the quart of potato salad. To be fair, at this hour in the morning there's only refrigerated food, but the only other time we'd been in this place was when we lied through our teeth to her parents and faked our first Thanksgiving meal together. Despite them being German immigrants living in Connecticut, and not usually doing the turkey thing, I've always felt they'd sniffed it out. But I wasn't the rock climber or the EDM DJ and so they played it cool. Her dad, only slightly inebriated, pretty much fessed to that in his wedding toast. To the one who rock climbed at least. Something about his gratitude for Mt. Olympus being in her rearview put Sascha's eyes in her lobster bisque.

There's decent drip up front. The small seating area has chairs over the tables and the woman at checkout says we're welcome to take one. We ask for a plastic spoon and sit on the bus bench outside trading potatoes and coffee. Sascha asks how I think my mom is managing.

"I can just picture her," she says as she puts a spoonful in my mouth before I can find the right answer. "I'm sure Darius is all about it."

"Thank you for this."

"Yeah," more to the air than to me.

My head is on the armrest and my ankles on her thighs, the wrought iron massaging the knot on the back of my head that's been there since I threw it against the rim of the tub after one of our first fights. Sascha moves the cuffs of my jeans and gently twists the hair on my shins.

"You could seriously donate this shit to chemo patients," she says.

I think of making a joke, something with fuck off, but close my eyes and wait for the spots.

I wake to the beeps of the unfolding handicap ramp, and to the apparition of a cinnamon-skinned woman in a purple-and-gold sequined bomber jacket and a padded chair. She is glittering, with a crumpled paper bag and an oxygen tank on her lap. The potato salad is nowhere to be seen.

The driver is shouting for this woman to stop. The hose of her tank is tangled in the door's hinge and I stumble up to help push the door back from the outside, my eyes at the level of the veins and flesh escaping her compression socks. When she is free, before she motors away, she squeezes my hand with a delicateness that takes me to the grandmother of an old friend.

I peek my head into the bus. Besides a couple taking up the whole last row and a man with enormous studio headphones, it's empty.

"Come on," turning to Sascha on the bench. Though she lived here nine years, this would be her first bus ride in LA. Definitely the first since we've been together. "I'm serious," as I dig behind the insurance cards to where I keep the cash for the tolls when we head north on I-95 to visit her family.

The driver flicks her wrist and I stand back so she can draw in the ramp. She's skinny and dark-haired, more an aged and disgruntled Hollywood film waitress than a bus driver. Sandra Bullock trying a deep character dive. Sascha would call her rode hard. I hand her five dollars but she demands exact change with the smoker's voice I'd expected. I ask if she can put what's left toward the next passenger and she looks into her fisheye mirror. "Go on now," refusing the money with a wink. "But," pointing to Sascha's coffee, "she'll have to throw that out."

I rode this same line three times a week in grad school. Like just about everything in the city, on the surface this bus is cleaner than most from back then, but the mosaic seats with their sporadic cigarette burns and petrified gum are the same. We pass the man with the headphones and stand at the back door. I slump to watch the street signs with my arm tight around Sascha's shoulder.

"I miss this dress," I tell her. I want to add that I like that it rides higher with the weight, how it looks on her legs, but she wouldn't believe me.

My mind sticks on the fourteen-hour layover in Charles de Gaulle as I made my way back to Los Angeles, to the empty apartment save for the water-worn bamboo dish rack with one unfamiliar mug.

I pull the cord too late. The next stop is three blocks past our car, but Sascha seems fine with it. We jump into the grass as the bus slows and the heel strap on her sandal breaks. She grabs me by the elbow while she pulls off both and we walk like this, her hand in the bend of my arm, alternating balding grass and concrete until we are driving back to the hotel.

'thresh-ˌhōld

The day after the planes found the buildings the aliens on the southwest corner of La Cienega and Pico were selling flags with their hot dogs. He wondered where they had come from. It was then he discovered the unmistakable taste of copper in his nostrils, that whispering wordless laughter that divides him from himself. Many years later, in an august South, when he was unable to identify the wretched of the earth for his wife, who so desperately wanted them gathered she carried him to the ER, it was suddenly a laughter in need of the ritual of naming.

The Deafman

*or fragments of the apocryphal book of Raphael of Nacogdoches
and his journey to the Mexican Sierra*

June 1971

The Mazatec boy and the black youth sit for some twenty-five minutes before the gathering crowd of university students begins to understand. The boy is dressed in linen brown with mud, and the other, somewhat older and thick-necked, in a Victorian collar to his Adam's apple, a large-brimmed black felt hat and suspenders. Even with the morning chill, the boy shows a dimple when he talks. One student must venture from below the steps of the entrance to the gymnasium where the two were found, bundled together against the damp, to find another from the Sierra. Of course, all wonder how the travelers got here. And about the odd pairing. But most are more concerned with the vitality of the two than the mystery. Strange people show up all the time, but these are menacing times, as news is still echoing in the city of the massacre of students in the capital six days before. Those in this crowd demonstrated in support of the reforms in the very same quad they now stand, but while there were police, there were no death squads. And though they have pored over *El Universal* each morning since last Thursday, looking for men with sticks and youths with mangled faces, they know the death toll from the capital will be worse than the press will ever be allowed to calculate. It was supposed to have been the day to celebrate the body and blood of Christ. And while last Sunday some of them were at mass, with demands that gods speak of this violence, here there are two bodies that were brought through something that they can tend to.

One of the students brings tejate from the vendor at the gates to help the boy tell his story in words that are sometimes difficult for the translator to understand, having the language of one brought to the city in the womb. The Deafman, the triangulated moniker for the boy's companion, drove them in a van the color of smoldering harvest until they ran out of petrol. They pushed the van far off the road and buried it in brush. He points to The Deafman's collared neck where the key hangs on twine made from cornhusks. He, the boy, exchanged their cargo—pine-oak boards, goat milk and sapote—for space in the back of mule-driven carts. They walked the last fifteen kilometers in the dark, following the glow of the lights from the university's quad that under federal order had been on through the nights since last Thursday. They found their dark corner to sleep before the students, those coming from far, began to walk in.

The boy was known to leave, he admits, to frustrate his elders, but always alone and never this far. This is the first he has seen of the city. He says that at this point his village will be whistling to the hills for him, and that he will try and find someone from near to his home and begin the return when the market clears in the days to come. The translator asks if he needs a place to sleep in the meantime and the boy says no, repeating that he will find someone truly from the Sierra, that the markets should be full of them. And this other? the translator asks. The boy is confident his friend will find his way. He is found, he says.

The Deafman sits silent, fingering the key around his neck, his felt hat pulled low to one side and his head turned toward the lightlessness of their cobbled refuge. One of the students, with greasy dark curls falling over his face, whispers in the translator's ear, urging him to ask of The Deafman's motives. Given the disheveled theatricality of the dark traveler's wardrobe, it is as if this student is reading Melville and thinking of Babo. The boy tells the translator that the teen who looks like a man does not speak. He is sure to slowly say that he has come of his own free will and that he considers his accomplice a friend. The skeptic takes a short and gnarled pencil hidden behind his ear and looks past the translator, pointing it at The Deafman. He asks in a raised voice where he is from, attempting to curry support, but he is punched in the arm and cursed silent.

The crowd of students, some sharing cigarettes and many with their books tied in leather for the rains, has more than doubled in size, as if the two strangers were jugglers or fire eaters. Though he knows they will not comprehend, the boy speaks to the crowd, telling them that the troupe of foreigners The Deafman came to the Sierra with may be following on foot. The translator begins to ask how he and The Deafman communicate but is tripped by the mention of a troupe. This word takes some minutes to get to. Given the rumors, it is of no surprise that the translator thinks the boy is talking of mercenaries making a march to the city. Though the boy insists that the foreigners were putting on a show, the translator is steadily unsure if this meaning is precise.

The translator asks if the men speak like him. The boy shakes his head. The translator asks if he is aware of the violence. Though the boy's village had been burned out of their lands three times since he could remember, he knows this is not what he is being asked. The translator tells him the story of the hawks being sent to kill the students. The boy thinks of his great grandmother and how she talks to the birds of the Sierra. This is how the death squads are known, the translator says to the boy's confusion, explaining that they, the boy and The Deafman, were thought to be lifeless bodies because of the way they were lying in the nook of the concrete stairs, as if they had tried to find shelter but were taken by the hawks. That they looked like the black-and-white photos they were searching for in *El Universal*. The boy insists that he and The Deafman are not ghosts.

May 1970

Raphael has come to the tree in Bed-Stuy after his morning shift in the
woodshop at The Lighthouse for the last three weeks. He had read the feature
in the *Times* about the woman who was organizing the neighborhood kids to
care for the greenery of Brooklyn. A reclamation of humanity. Incredulous,
he came when he heard that a southern magnolia, somehow sheltered against
the cold by a brownstone, has survived for decades, hundreds of miles from its
intended ground. The tree reminds him of the good things from East Texas that
he had not run from, of how his mother would send him to collect petals that
she would soak and boil down to make her summer perfume.

With June coming the branches are starting to firm. He is here today, with
his usual roast beef and 7 Up, for cuttings to add to his makeshift arboretum
on the roof of his loft where he is collecting the species of the city. He climbs
just below the freshest branches, hangs his knapsack with his pruning knife on a
knob of the trunk and hides among the blooms to eat his lunch. All of six-foot-
three with his rosy skin, Roman nose and gangly limbs, his mother had called
him her flamingo. But besides the occasional passerby looking into the tree and
a few children even waving, most have not bothered to notice him. Maybe, he
thinks, he will return with a sack for petals to fill the bowls he has been teaching
his blind students to make on the lathe from scrap wood. When he balances
his sandwich on the branch to sip his soda, he can see the young black boys
with watering cans making their rounds in the park across the street. He thinks
about the telegram to his father asking for tuition that he can no longer delay
because, though he dropped out in October, the rent is two months past due.
When he has not been volunteering in the woodshop or sitting in trees, he has
been making crude drawings of sets and scenes, sticking them to the sheetrock
with chewed gum and running them with his growing following of amateur
talent.

Before the screams reach him, he believes the children with the watering
cans are playing a game, running as kids do when the sun comes after such a

harsh winter. Then he sees the torrent of black flesh, and the police with billy clubs and white helmets, his soda tumbling through the branches as the blacks split the fountain and dart through the trees that lead to the street. He is still unbelieving until one of the officers catches an older boy, wearing shorts and running slower than the rest, and throws him to the ground by the throat. The other police, Raphael counts four, turn to the circling crowd, not yet using their clubs or their guns. From his height he can see more sprinting from the precinct just beyond the park as a woman cursing in howls is being held back from the vortex, the crowd trying to keep her from the helmeted men. For an instant she is pulled just enough for him to see the face of the boy. Raphael hears the splintering of bone, though he knows that with the distance this is an invention. A mounted officer trots the perimeter, daring the stragglers to come any closer. When the police from the station arrive, the horseman splits the crowd so they may enter. As the circle widens, Raphael can see that the boy is tied with a line of rope and being dragged by his feet to the horse, can see the officer dismounting to help the others secure the limp body like a sack of flour to the horse's croup. The woman struggles free from the grip of an officer and grabs the belt of the saddle, trying to lift the head of the boy, perhaps her boy, as the officers strike her sacrum. It is not like it was with the boy. They slowly wind up and take turns, as if they are placing bets on who will be the first to dislodge her. Falling, she manages to kick her shoeless heel square into the nose of one of the officers. He wipes the blood and licks it from his wrist with a smile. The rest know to simply let loose their grip as he begins to swing with blows that break apart the underwire of her bra. When he has tired the others undress her with what, to Raphael, is a peculiar violence, slapping at her bleeding breasts as they continue to pin her down. The one who took the heel walks to the horse where the tied boy, scarlet running through his matted and unevenly cut hair, has not regained consciousness. With a knife from his belt he cuts the lobe of an ear and feeds it to the woman, forcing her mouth and nose shut. The trained horse does not move, only shifts slightly so the boy's butchered head may loll and let more blood. When a police car arrives, crawling through the crowd on the dirt walk of the park, demonstrating no need for sirens or flashing lights, a man throws a soda bottle that merely bursts on the rubber of the tire. Another, a woman in a turquoise dress and black flats who may have just been unlucky enough to pass through the park on her way back to an office after lunch, slaps the hood until the officer who was on the horse fires his gun at the light post just above her head. At the shattering of glass, the woman and the crowd begin to run again, away from the two beaten black bodies. It takes five officers to shackle and carry the naked woman to the backseat. This time, she turns her head away as they pass the horse that carries the boy. Some in the broken crowd steady themselves on the concrete rim of the fountain while others hold children. When the horse begins its saunter, following the car the two blocks to the precinct, a young girl appears to collect the woman's bloodied flowered shift from the street. Maybe this evening or in the morning they will come together and throw stones at the glass doors of the precinct. But now, the noises of the woman the strange silence of the boy the frenzied yet rehearsed steps of the crowd the breath of the horse, all of it is gone. And Raphael has no alphabet for what he has seen. He does not remember descending from his southern magnolia or boarding the train or opening the door to his nearly abandoned building or climbing the stairs to his loft. All he knows is that now it is dark and drizzling and he is naked, with a woman's wail buried in him. It takes his mind to when he was eight and his father forced him to go raccoon hunting the week after his mother died. It'll straighten him out, he heard his father say on the phone, maybe talking to his aunt in Oklahoma, before he knocked on his bedroom door. By the knock he knew his father meant to be tender, that he had borrowed the neighbor's hound and they would go into the forest behind the house. Raphael's job was to hold the hound. He remembers that it took him all ways and that he tripped over the root of a cedar elm and bit his lip. His father fired one shot that day and waited as the raccoon lost its life, taking the leash so Raphael could sit on the ground and plug his ears and look away. His father didn't even hunt, just brought the animal in a grain sack to the neighbor who fed the meat to his dog.

Raphael prepares his words as he is led to the aquarium of steel and chipped paint that is the Brooklyn House of Detention's empty cafeteria, passing a window where a shirtless man with hair to his nipples stares at him while being made to grip a metal table by someone out of view. Raphael is pointed to one of the bolted benches surrounding the cafeteria's round tables and told the boy's case manager is with another detainee and will be along shortly.

Unsure of who else may be peering at him, he looks to his hands, thinking about his morning's journey, following the path of the police car from the day before, standing where the boy had been, where excrement from the horse had been trampled and remains, the rain light enough to make the blood spilled run but not to disappear it, the empty clearing in the park where the neighbors usually milled about as he watched from his perch.

This morning he grabbed the front section from one of the old newspapers stacked by his door, using that to shield his head from the rain until it gave way. News on the first color images of Earth from space but nothing that could intuit the cataclysm in Tompkins Park he witnessed yesterday. He was taken in by the rain as he looked toward the bridge where the sun broke through, thinking about how an image, one's body from above, his only way of remembering yesterday, can produce an end of safety. And before a divine compulsion led him to the 79th Precinct to see about the boy, he sat on the lip of the fountain with the presence of the girl who had collected the flowered shift. During the whole confusion she had sat calmly. He did not see that yesterday. So calmly he now wonders if he imagined her, imagined her moving to collect the soiled clothing of the woman.

The officer behind the yellowed glass at the precinct had told him little, only that the boy was no longer there, that he was alive but was taken to the detention center in the early hours of the morning. When Raphael asked after the boy's name, he was told he came with no name and no kin and that the boy would not talk. And the woman? Raphael asked. The one who was brought in with the boy? I know nothing of nothing this officer told him.

Raphael hears the case manager emerge from a closed door, speaking softly to a guard. He stands to shake hands but the graying crew-cut man only nods and squints as he digs a tobacco pouch out of his blue slacks. He sits opposite Raphael, separating the stems and filling his paper.

"I was directed here by the 79th," Raphael says, as if he had been given approval, sliding his elbows from the table so as not to crowd. The man offers to roll him one but Raphael knows this would betray his nerves.

"Your relation to this boy?" flicking a tobacco leaf from his tie before taking a disheveled memo pad from his shirt pocket.

"An assistant of mine at The Lighthouse."

"As in the school for the blind?"

"Yes."

"I had a cousin who was blind but that was years back. Before places like that," stopping his writing to show a wrinkled smile. "But the negro's not blind."

"Theo," Raphael says, the name of the son of his father's housekeeper that he practiced on the train. "Theodore Carter. He helps me organize woodworking projects with the students."

"Raphael, right?

"Yes."

"Let me get it out front, they tell me you want to see him but I can't do that."

"But he's done nothing wrong."

He flips a page from his pad and brings it to his eyes: "*Building shrines for dead niggers all over Brooklyn…claiming the police right killed niggers…stirring shit up,*" looking up. "That's what the law tells us."

"I don't know anything about shrines, but I can assure you that Theo is not that person."

"You can assure me? Let me guess, you're voting for Mailer?"

"He was with me."

"Just fucking with you, but I'm right, right?"

"We'd taken a student home and were on our way to the train when…all I'm saying is there's been a mistake and I can help."

"He won't talk to us. We can't help him if he doesn't talk."

"He's a deaf-mute," an improvisation somehow managed without hesitation. "Look how he watches your mouth."

Without taking his eyes from Raphael he mashes his cigarette on the table and puts it back in with the loose tobacco.

"Look, no formal charges are being processed, but if his family isn't found we will have no choice but to transfer him to long-term juvenile detention. We're full up."

Raphael is familiar with this nightmare. Not just from the papers but with a few kids from The Lighthouse having spent time at Spofford.

"And what's happened to his mother?"

"Mother?"

"Theo's mother. The woman they arrested with him."

"Not in the file that she had any relation, and nothing about her being a mother. But if you're really that inquisitive, she is no longer with us."

Stuttering, he again asks if he can see the boy and is given the detail of an ongoing stay in the infirmary. With a tear running through his throat he invents for Theo a sister in North Carolina and claims he can get him to her. The case manager stares beyond Raphael's shoulder as he wipes the ash from the polished, scratched steel table, tells him to come back noon the day after next, though he can make no promises.

Raphael jumps at the jangle of keys to find Charlotte at the door with a cakebox and Kris on the landing just below, struggling with her suitcase.

"You said medium, right?" Kris yells, out of breath from carrying the suitcase the four flights.

He waves her silent and half closes the door behind him before running down the steps to help.

"I just took some from my brother's closet," she says.

"It'll be fine."

She wipes the sweat from her chest with her red knit beanie and kisses him on the forehead. The three quietly enter the loft and tiptoe to the far wall of the immense, still-unfinished space. Raphael points to the corner where he has pulled his mattress and pinned a bed sheet between the wooden pillars for the boy. He pours them tea and they sit at the window that looks from Wooster toward Prince. Charlotte slices her banana bread and brings the peanut butter.

"How was upstate?" Raphael asks.

"Same shit," Kris says. "My parents gave us some money. They say hello. And I couldn't find bunny ears, but I did get an old Robin Hood hat from the thrift shop."

"I'm of the mind to go with the goats now."

"Papier-mâché?" Kris says above a whisper before catching herself. "In this heat?"

Raphael leans to the window, looks down the littered street below, following a spectacled man with a shirt and tie carrying a double bass on his back. The man stops to roll his sleeves and rest against the brick wall just below them.

"And he came with nothing?" Charlotte asks.

"Who?"

She throws her chin to the corner where the boy supposedly sleeps.

"Barely clothed. I laid Kris's nightshirt by the bed with two glasses of water."

From here Raphael can only go backward, recounting the guards walking the boy to the street and helping him into the cab, him not knowing what the case manager had told the boy or if he had been sedated. That he had stayed in the front seat and told the boy as they crossed the river that he would help to find his family, and said no more until he offered his arm to lead him by the elbow up the stairs. That in the silence of the night and the morning he has sat on the couch Charlotte sleeps on when she crashes, wondering if the boy judged him sincere or if it was just that he knew wherever he had been taken was better than the hole he had been placed in.

"We could take him back to the park," Kris says. "Surely someone would recognize him."

"I've thought about that. But can you imagine?"

"A photo," Kris says. "Maybe we can take a photo."

"And carry it around the whole of Brooklyn?"

"We can post a bunch. Around the precinct, the park. I've a friend with a lab."

"I think tomorrow I'll take him to the doctor we send my students to."

"Well, I'll stay at Char's till you get this sorted."

"You can't just keep him here, Raphael," Charlotte finally puts in.

"He needs to convalesce. Then he can tell us what to do."

"Convalesce?" Kris laughs out, poking at the formalities that Raphael brought from Texas and has yet to discard.

The three hush their voices when the curtain opens, knowing it is not a gust, the rain and breezes of the last days having passed. The boy stands in the oversized undershirt and cut hospital greens he left the station in. They see no blood and most of the bruising is lost in his skin. Raphael waits for the boy he had conjured without words to speak, but the boy turns from them to the opposite window ledge where Raphael keeps the youngest seedlings in water, fixated on a chipped highball glass with a cutting from the wind-blown branch of a London Plane lying in Raphael's path as he walked past Sara Roosevelt Park on his way home from The Lighthouse last week. "There's food," Raphael interrupts from behind with a shaky faith in his own kindness, pointing to the loaf Charlotte left in the kitchen. The boy is gracious and follows Raphael's welcome to the upturned and paint-speckled wooden door that has become their table, waits as he is brought the peanut butter. They watch him eat. As he stoops his shoulders to finger a crumb to his mouth, he turns his head just enough for Kris to see.

Raphael took his first shift at The Lighthouse since the park, leaving the boy at the window with his reverence for the cutting, sketching not the roots but the ashes of cinnamon spread on the water, untangling the sutures growing from the garnet crystals that are the remains of his ear.

"Are you disturbed?"

"Is that what art is supposed to do?"

"Does that make you any less whatever the hell you are?"

Though she is unsure of the texture of Lucie's error, Kris smiles over her mug of bitter coffee. Owen and Charlotte are too concerned with their blocking to take an interest in Raphael's now familiar rising voice.

"Are you crying?" Raphael starts again after a petulant glare. Lucie begins a mumble, not aware that she is still to be without words.

Before leaving her in a heap and escaping through the rough-cut hole in the sheet metal of the abandoned grain silo to smoke where the land meets the woods, Raphael looks to Owen and Charlotte, who have by now raised their heads. They know to continue. As has been the case in the months since Raphael assumed guardianship, Theo, as Raphael has had to name him, sits above them all on the top of his wooden platform, drawing with his head down before he must eat and go to the tents to sleep.

The ragged ensemble has been squatting in the mountains of Oaxaca for eleven days now. It was past midnight on a Wednesday two months ago when Raphael gathered Kris, Owen and Charlotte under a mist of low clouds on the roof of his loft. In the last year, with Theo under his charge and the troop's improvisational rehearsals intensifying, he has taken to calling this space The Cave. He revealed the vision that led them to the south of Mexico, meandering about how he was on the cusp of penetrating the heart of the work that brought them together just months prior, his second organized foray into anything resembling theater. He told them that, when he could not sleep, he remembered a comment from a high school class in Nacogdoches, Texas about an indigenous community that whistled across mountains to communicate. He told them that the work they are doing is about distance and darkness, that Theo and his drawings brought him to this and Mexico would carry them through it. And so, in two rust-orange Dodge campers rented with the last of the money begged from his father, they traveled from a place named by those who came before for its many hills to another for the trees they saw every day. Lucie, a friend of Owen's since high school in South Carolina, met them at a bus depot outside of Toledo. When they discovered the remote silo, Raphael was drawn to the acoustics of the galvanized steel, and so they have spent the early days of June camped here, refining the silent prologue in ten-hour rehearsals.

Despite the fact that Theo has made it his mission to collect the remnants of silage in his empty boxes of lemon candy, when Lucie finds her feet she still must peel amaranth from her wet cheeks. Kris sets her mug on the soft, chocolate dirt and crosses the stage Raphael has marked with fallen limbs to place a hand on the fragile bone of Lucie's shoulder. Before Lucie folds again, Kris takes her hand and walks her outside.

Raphael turns from his distance to see Kris assuring him with her eyes as she guides Lucie to the ground where they lay on their backs. Brash as Raphael might be, Kris tells Lucie, she knows his explosions to be guided by a rare honesty and not an abusiveness born of insecurity. She kisses her temple and, as Raphael had done with her, asks her to pick a cloud in the early evening sky. She has her point to it, tells her to watch it dance. They lay like this until the trees cover the sun. Raphael is pleased and comes to sit beside them. When they return to the silo Lucie understands the pace and lightness with which she is expected to move.

While the others were running the prologue, Owen took the trip an hour north to Tajao with the cherubic young son of the nearby village chief in search of stew meat and psychedelic mushrooms. The Mazatec boy had shown up in their camp the day after they arrived with a bag of roasted tree nuts, pointed them to the spring when he saw them boiling their water. Owen asks for favors in gestures and pays him in quarters. He learned the name for the tea in the boy's language before they left New York and brought a picture ripped from the pages of National Geographic.

Me sleeping beneath the foliage-covered lean-to / K&L make preparations for celebratory meal—L whittling feather sticks K working a potato peeler / Char across the stage folds paper [Theo drops from his sky] with old kitchen knife and licks the edge, tears precise fuzzy squares like grade school / K watches Char, now blindly with the peeler, keeps time / When the flesh is exhausted, sets it on the ground, collects the scraps, places them in metal bucket between her feet

The Mazatec boy and the black youth, still dressed in his costume from the day's rehearsal, sit with their backs against the trunk of a pine-oak, throwing foraged stones into a clay pot, feeling the hollow thump and watching as the ensemble settles around the fire after walking the forest. Caught in a hysterical vision, Raphael takes off his shoes to walk the path to the village and lay restless on the doormat of the house at the furthest edge. The rest sleep by the embers.

Slipping out of her dreams for distant thunders and fireflies, Charlotte rolls over to the two still throwing their stones, unable to make sense of the sound and the passage of time. The one she calls Theo stands and walks to her, covers her with the sweater she had peeled off hours before, then walks to the back gate of the first van, leaning against it to suffocate the sound of the latch, searching under the carpeted trunk for the jack and lug wrench. He smiles at the boy as if to say goodbye, but the boy comes to him.

They raise the van, sweat sliding off the boy's eyelashes as he struggles in silence to help loosen the lug nuts. They send the tires into the ravine, the echo of worn rubber in the air and on their hands. The black youth starts to detach the plastic jugs of petrol but the noise rises above the toads, instead takes the knife tucked in his waist and slides it into each. The boy follows him to the van that stores the wood and provisions, watches him open the driver's door and feel for the mirror and the hanging key. Unsetting the brake, the black youth looks again to the boy before they roll, lightless.

An Apparent Horizon

———————————————

~~everything is~~ (in) erasure Fred

Moten

y no hay remedio

Francisco Goya

———————————————

The sun has yet to come but predawn has brought its gray, and the light from Marley Gillette's trailer still throws her shape on the pale orange curtains over the sink. She is at her desk, sipping from a cup and reading what looks to be a newspaper. Or a map. She has opened it, turned to another section and compacted it once more.

She opens the corrugated metal door. Sock footed, she reaches under the stairs for the Ziploc bags that hold her boots and without a flashlight walks, two empty one-gallon jugs to a hand, around the potted rosemary at the foot of her stairs toward where she knows there to be a submerged rainwater tank at the nearest corner of her acre plot of desert land, land that she has spent almost the past two years cultivating in the manner of the Hohokam after leaving an academic research fellowship devoted to their study.

Derrick has stationed himself in a tent thirty feet away for ten days, observing and reporting on her hunger strike. He had announced her harvests on his blog and its various sinews, bringing volunteers from all over the state to see the garden and deliver its food to shelters along the Central Coast. A missionary is how she is most often described in such spaces. When she first came with her truck and small trailer she was left alone, thought to be one of the many palatable itinerants who dot the landscape in small campers and mind their own, come and go. But the desert belongs to the Bureau of Land Management and three weeks ago she was given an injunction to vacate signed by the state director and stamped by the governor's office.

It is a short rainy season and the sandy soil does not hold. The first winter she bought two water tanks and paid three day laborers outside the Home Depot in Atascadero to dig through the night. By the first harvest, before anyone of consequence had noticed her, she had buried a third. The agents came, she denied the planting and they have been in battle ever since, the garden now wild with the summer crop going to seed and the periphery having outgrown the supply altogether. A section of the drip line nearest the lone viable tank has been dug up, severed and plugged, and this is where she gets at what is left. It is the system's only mark above ground. She comes to her knees to blow air to the sponged hose, swallows a mouthful of dirt and water and starts with the first jug. Less than half is full when the water slows. She seems to prepare to blow again but nothing comes, and no effort is made to conceal the hose.

"No water?" shouts Derrick. He has unfolded a low-lying beach chair and is boiling his coffee on the one-burner propane stove. She cups her hand to her ear. He points to the jugs. "Surprised it took this long," he says. Mar shakes her head and laughs, he thinks, climbs the three steps of her trailer and places the water-bearing jug inside the door.

Derrick mixes the crystals of his coffee with a finger as he walks toward Mar. "Gonna breakfast with the wife and kid," loudly for the distance and the emptiness. "I'll bring some back. In the meantime, I have a two-liter in the cooler. I don't need it," with an exaggerated slurp. "This might as well be water."

Mar only asks him to spare some cooler water for the rosemary she planted with her father's ashes when she had first arrived in the desert. He sets the coffee on the small white plastic folding table they have placed between his tent and her trailer and walks to a shade constructed with his daughter's light-green bed sheet and PVC piping. "Now don't go drinking this," chuckling as he returns with a full jug. He suggests she mark it, searches the pocket of his cutoff camouflage shorts to find a ballpoint.

Inside, she pours what water she managed from the tank into a large glass decanter and adds the purification tablets. Staring at the mountains over her cluttered desk, she rubs her fingers over the thick and textured glass of its lip. Derrick knocks lightly on the screen door and calls her name, not realizing until his face touches the mesh that she is less than an arm's length away. She turns slowly. "Here's that bottle." Sensing the rise of another refusal, "Hell, use it for the rosemary." He can see the *Weekly*, the one with his story, turned to the Letters section and on the floor. "You say those are wheat fields?" squinting at the framed picture on her desk. "In Los Angeles?"

"Did I say wheat?" reaching without moving her feet for the one photo she has kept of her and her father. "Wild brush. Looks like wheat with the blur doesn't it?" She tilts the picture in his direction. "It's Century City. Nothing but buildings now. Not in 1975, just those few in the background." They had an almost identical exchange when he first arrived on the third day of the hunger strike, the last time she invited him into her trailer, when they had agreed to let the past be the past and when he was able to convince her that not only would her story be more powerful if he camped out with her but that its believability hinged on whether he could vouch for, as he phrased it, the lack of nourishment.

"My little one doesn't smile in pictures," he says.

"Will you call those two grad students when you go to town?"

"My editor too. Small chance the day fourteen piece will run in LA and New York. But we'll need pictures."

She suggests tomorrow or the day after, crossing her arms and looking to the small solar generator. "Can you help? I want to catch more of the early sun. Just a few feet and turn the panels."

"I'll bring an extension from the house. That way we could pull it further out and leave it. Maybe even put it up in the bed. Your truck ain't going nowhere."

"I imagine she's rooting against me." He removes his brown-meshed baseball cap and squeezes the bill. "Your wife."

"Sometimes I know she regrets she didn't marry a plumber."

Mar disappears into the trailer, returning with a ten-dollar bill that has been neatly folded in quarters. "For that water."

"Absolutely not."

"Can you at least burn your story onto my thumb drive?"

"That, I can do." His loose curls hang over his ears as he looks down. "I'm gonna need a number for the next story. They're asking for it. I was thinking I'd say fifteen."

"Fifteen?"

"Pounds."

"Closer to twenty would be my guess."

"And I was thinking I'd bring my daughter up to spend the night with me today. Quiet kid, I promise." Mar's eyes move to a red-shouldered hawk floating in the sky above his head. A gust of wind blows her rose-colored blouse and Derrick can see the loose-fitting ribbed tank top beneath. "That'd be alright?"

"She could be a banshee for all I care."

The sun has broken over the low rolling mountains that are the eastern border of the plain. Waiting for the generator to charge, Mar reads the notes taken on scraps of paper over the last three days. Two honks and the grumble of Derrick's muffler trail in the desert. She opens her laptop and pauses at her diary's first entry: *what is brown is green.* She scrolls to the end of the near eight-hundred-page document and starts typing the notes chronologically. When she throws the first day's entries in the copper bin, she notices a stream of ascending ants two inches thick on the cabinet beneath the sink. A to-be-washed pair of underwear that had hung from the faucet has fallen into the basin and is covered with the ants maneuvering the purple satin folds and collecting, crawling over each other, in the cotton crotch that had been spotted with blood.

She reaches for her vinegar spray on the sill. While they are not dying, they are slowing. Half of the water from Derrick's clean liter fills a salad bowl and she pushes the underwear around with a fork as the still-living struggle around the dead, attempting the swim to the ridge in water filled with traces of her blood. She sprays what to the ants must register as a cataract, watches it float in bubbles and reflect the sun, and forks the underwear to the light to see that they have eaten portions of the fabric. She opens the window and throws them to the ground outside. In an hour, when they have dried, she adds them to the copper bin and puts rubbing alcohol and a match to the pile.

Derrick knocks on the door to Mar's trailer. She opens it to find two gallons on her top step and him returning to his car. "Your daughter?"

"The wife didn't think it was the brightest idea." Mar drags the water inside one at a time. "I spoke to the two grad students. They're from Michigan. I don't know why I thought Texas," with the last gallon swinging in his left hand.

"Are they planning to starve themselves?"

"I didn't ask. But I did call the folks at Channel 6. They want to come tomorrow and shoot with the morning light. I told them around ten but I couldn't guarantee they'd talk to you."

"Not really a place for a kid anyway."

"Said she might bring her up for a few hours next Saturday. But I think she was just saying it."

Sometime after three o'clock she fills her laundry bucket with water and washes out a white blouse and tan shorts. They are on the line in time for the late-afternoon sun. Arranging her folding chair by the rosemary, she rubs its needles and reads the book her mother sent up last Christmas.

She wakes up with the sun on her and Derrick reading a distance away at the table that divides their makeshift compound, his cap pulled low over his sunglasses. When she gets up to check her clothes, he raises his head from the paper. He marvels at how, through whatever feat of shade and slather, she has maintained such fair skin. She reverses the shorts and clips them again, ducks the line and, despite her fatigue, comes to share the table, sets her book and wipes the sweat from her upper lip. In the last few days they have moved away from the habit, for her growing weakness he assumes, of reading here in silence just after the sun has quit. He pushes his aluminum water bottle toward her. She collects the condensation, rubbing it behind her ears.

"You know, we drink water?" She smiles, takes a small sip and returns it to his side of the table that is pocked with long-cured crayon wax. Derrick is reading a newspaper that he brought up from his trip home. "Well, for what it's worth, my Padres lost to your Dodgers in the ninth and now we're four games out." He throws the paper between them. "So, thank you." He lifts his cap enough to get at an itch on his scalp, picks up her book. "I see you are still reading about the Lost Ones."

"The Lost Boys."

He reads her mother's note. "Bear? Is that you? Get the fuck out of here. Your mother says that each book pays for a brick in this guy's village."

"It's horrifying and sleep inducing at the same time." She lunges for the book but he holds it away.

"Does your mother's heart always bleed, or just at Christmas?"

She flicks an aqua-green fragment she had been digging at. In all the space it miraculously lands on his sun-worn cheek.

"So you really haven't been home to LA since you came out here? I can't wrap my head around that. Was thinking on that on my way back from seeing my little one."

"Not sure what you mean."

"In a sentence, what's this about for you?"

"What about you? How did you end up here? Not here, Paso."

"My wife's family. It's not Southern California but not the worst. She's close with her family. My little one." He closes Mar's book. "But nobody wants to follow me around."

"I didn't ask for this."

"I mean, the easy answer would be to write, and I have, that you represent the best in us, that you appeal to the off-the-grid zeitgeist sponsored by Whole Foods. But you aren't selling bricks." He puts the sports section back in its place. "If I can speak honestly," he says. "The first time I emailed you I knew I was attracted to you. Not that it wasn't tied up with everything you had done. It was the picture of you in the *Times*."

"I knew you were trying to fuck me from the start," pausing before asking for the Calendar section.

"No more lions?" is all Derrick can summon before they resume an accustomed silence. But the sun will not set for two more hours and she excuses herself, touching her still-wet shorts on the line as she continues to her trailer.

Derrick is using Mar's binoculars to survey the dwindling thrush when he begins to track the noiseless wobble of the Channel 6 van's satellite as it comes off the highway to the uneven road.

"Gillette," knocking with an ear to the door. Though her shoes are sealed in their Ziploc bags beneath the steps he circles the trailer to see if she has escaped to the garden. The curtain on the window above her writing desk has been pulled back. He stands on the tire, brings his lashes to the dust of the screen to discover her face first on the floor. The door was unlocked. He turns her, feels the rough mapping of the burlap mat on her cheek. Two fingers find her throat.

Derrick pulls her blouse off the line and wildly flags the news van. The driver sips from his station-issued travel mug, slowly rolling down his window. "Can I not park here?" over the van's radio.

"She's passed out. Have an ambulance meet us at the highway," yelling as he looks over the lap of the driver to a confused kid not yet out of his teens and waves him to follow. The boy sprints to catch up with Derrick at the steps to the trailer, is out of breath when he sees Mar's body. He is either uninterested or incapable of entering. "Help me carry her to my car," touching the boy's shoulder. "You take the legs."

The boy, whom Derrick figures as an intern, switches her feet to one arm to open the car door. Derrick points with his chin but the boy is helpless to understand. "Set them down and go around." Derrick attempts to sit gently and still Mar's head on his lap, but it rolls to his belly. The boy stands awkwardly. "The keys are on the dash. Run and grab her shoes from under the porch."

The boy is intent on running the car in second. The rising dust makes it difficult to see and he plays with the wipers until the water sprays. But it is only

128

worse and he must drive leaning to find a gap in the muddied windshield.

Only fifteen minutes pass before the ambulance arrives. Derrick's left leg is asleep. Her collarbone is cool to his touch though the dry heat is arriving. Somehow, her dried-crisp blouse, now covered with dirt, is still in his fist. He removes his sweatshirt arms first and covers her chest, licks his palm and places it below her nose as two blue-jumpsuited men dismount from the ambulance.

The cameraman had filmed the ambulance's approach and is now filming the men. With his free hand he directs them to the car. One secures Mar's head while Derrick extricates himself. "I understand she has not ingested anything in days," a crashing and Derrick glances over to the other who has thrown the gurney to the highway. He explains the hunger strike. When they ask his relation, he describes himself as a friend. They handle her firmly. On the gurney they force the eyelids. Derrick is certain he has seen Mar move.

"What can you tell?" he asks.

"She needs fluids."

"Can I ride with you?"

"Just one of you. No cameras."

"They're not coming."

Derrick quickly parks his car further off the shoulder and grabs a notebook from his glovebox. Mar is rolled into the ambulance where they begin to tug at her arm, attempting to find agreement as to which vein will take the IV, pausing to tell the hovering cameraman that he cannot film inside the vehicle. Derrick rises from the jumpseat, waving his arms to double the point. The gurney carrier thinks he can insert it in the jugular. He keeps saying it can be done. "No way, man," says the other. Their tone is light and they finally decide on the ankle. Turning away as the blood comes, Derrick wonders if this would have gone on if he were not there, if one or the other would have wagered a bottle of liquor.

Mar stares at the machine dripping electrolytes into her veins as Derrick sleeps with his feet resting on a magazine rack. In the space of a few minutes she has balled a portion of the sheet and pulled against it to move her hand to the bedside table where the foil on the plastic orange juice container has been peeled back by the nurse. She backhands it to the floor and Derrick snorts himself awake. She moans something that Derrick can neither understand nor intuit. Her mouth is dry and caked. He steps over the spilled juice and squats next to the breathing and beeping machine, lowers the rail to sit with her and rubs her thigh through the sheet. Her arm falls to his. Derrick imagines what she might be attempting.

"They wouldn't put you in the truck without the IV," he says.

Mar laughs, he thinks, and turns her head.

He crosses the room to the plant-less window with thick curtains more appropriate for the motel just off the road a half mile up. Mar has shut her eyes. He is sure she would have the same judgment. In their short time together he knows that, as much as she loved this place, the nature of it, she never stopped judging the men and manmade things that populated its surroundings. Even him, he knew, despite her many soft rejections of his intimacy. After a time, a small cough.

The nurse wakes Derrick with a hand on his bicep, looks toward the sleeping Mar and points to the darkened corridor. She is skinny and not five feet tall, wears a blue smock with faded white clouds and rainbows. "Some people came to see her," she says. Derrick looks down the empty hallway. "I sent them to the lobby. She is not allowed more than one overnight visitor."

"Who?"

"One guy had a camera. A couple more in suits. They said they come from the government. Only one was talking. Just like that, *we come from the government*. I told him he could come back for general visiting hours at nine."

"Was there a boy?"

"A boy?"

"A teenager. Gangly."

"No."

Sometime before five Derrick's phone vibrates in his pocket. A text from his wife. Mar is already up, moved to a wheelchair and placed by the window. She is wearing his red sweatshirt that he had covered her with when this ordeal started and is wrapped in a fleece blanket. Her shoes are on and she holds a muffin from the vending machine, rubbing the top and seeming to contemplate the grease on her finger. Derrick drinks from the sink and scrubs the grime from his teeth with a stiff paper towel.

The light above the nursing station by the elevator is the only light on the floor. The nurse stops reading when she hears the footrest bang against the doorframe and points him to the service elevator at the opposite end.

"This will take you right down to the parking structure without going through the lobby. The taxi should be waiting." She crouches to address Mar and hands her a brown paper bag and a bottle of water. "You be good to yourself."

They stay on their respective sides of the slick leather backseat, heads pressed to the windows. Only when they are approaching the service road, after Derrick tells the driver to be on the lookout for an Accord on the left shoulder, does she turn and speak.

"Thank you."

The sky is gray again and Derrick pulls at the stubble on his chin. He pays for the cab and walks Mar to his car as she wraps the slack from the blanket. The battery is dead, the cab already a ways down the road. He checks the instruments and realizes the intern must have accidentally turned on the lights in his fit with the wipers, mutters a curse and reaches into his jeans for his phone.

"I'll walk for service. Have him called back."

He is halfway out when Mar gets his attention by slapping her hand on the center console. "Let's walk in."

"Too cold, too far."

"The chill will be gone in a few. We can watch the sun," bringing the water bottle to her lips and closing her eyes.

"I will miss it at this time," she says to him or to herself at the first hint of gold. "I'm OK. Come on."

"Stop," he says lightly. "Let me push it at least. It's a slight downhill, we'll take it as far as it goes." She settles back into her seat and lets him do what he feels he must.

He strains to walk while holding the steering wheel and the door frame, pulls up a quarter mile short of her trailer. She touches his hand as he sets the brake. "We'll go slow," she says.

They stop and sit on a rock. When Derrick first was here observing, she would walk out to this rock every morning as the sun was rising. He talks to fill the space, suggests that the news folks will make their way soon. Once they get to the trailer, she turns and sits down on the steps to untie her shoes. "When they come, tell them it's over and make them leave."

131

Mar exits the early-morning, energy-conserving darkness of Ralphs to find a dry wind and the cab driver parked in front. With her instruction he travels up La Brea where it curves into Franklin. His friendly chatter that had filled the car ride from the Greyhound station to the supermarket, to which Mar had responded in polite one-word answers, stops when he turns up the hill. At the second stop sign, when Franklin is no longer a visible landmark behind him, he hunches over the wheel and looks up to read the street sign obscured by an overhanging tree branch. A silver Porsche wheels around him. He playfully shakes his fist but it is already around the next bend. He begins again his crawl up the hill, in the rearview offering an apology with his eyes.

"Where are you from?" Mar asks with a smile.

He tries to relax into his seat. "Where do you think?"

"Africa?" pointing to the flag that hangs from the mirror. "I can't recognize the colors."

"Ethiopia," showing a dimple.

The sign at the bottom of her hill reads *Private Please Sound Horn* and he announces himself in this manner every few feet. Mar takes out four twenty-dollar bills, folds them together and spins them along her knuckles while he pulls into the driveway. She suggests that he reverse so that he may pull further to the right. "It doesn't look like it, but it'll be easier to get out," she says.

When he has made it to the very top, he looks in all three mirrors. "Much easier," setting the foot brake with a jerk and springing from the cab. But Mar has exited and is leaning in to retrieve a small plastic filing box and the potted rosemary that she has carried from the plain in a black trash bag. The driver offers his hand but Mar only asks for her duffel from the trunk.

"Here's fine," pointing to her feet where she has placed her filing box, handing him the folded bills. She waits until he has slunk back into his seat and made a note on a pad he keeps stuck to the dash. "Are you OK leaving?" He rolls down the window, unsure of what she is asking. "Just keep turning downhill and you'll be fine." She waits as he descends the private road, honking now only at each curve. When she imagines he is letting himself onto the main road she turns to face the house, expecting the yard to be untidy. This is unreasonable, she knows, as she herself mailed the checks each month to Teddy and Marta to keep to their duties.

She walks down the driveway steps and through the terracotta path to the front door. It is September and the dry heat has lingered. The pine needles are falling brown but most have been blown from the walkway and from the base of the large tree. Yesterday or perhaps this morning. She sets the rosemary down on the welcome mat and returns for the rest, passing the front windows and looking into the dining room only to find the view blocked by cream-colored curtains. She vaguely remembers a letter sent over a year ago by Marta that she had read and threw away without response. New owners had moved in next door and had destroyed the existing house to erect a new one that her father had protested and that now towers over her backyard. Marta expressed concern that just any construction worker could have a free look into the house.

The keys were her father's, on the Boulder Dad keychain she had given him when she started grad school some ten years back. As the door swings, she is greeted by an odor of Pine Sol so thick it is nearly suffocating. She lets in the dry air and takes the bags to the dining room, passing the den without a glance. With Marta's curtains the room is dark. She feels the texture and weight of the middle panel, twisting her head to read the label and pulling it back to bring the light. She forces the wooden-framed window halfway. It is swollen and warped by years of weather and will go no further. The curtains sway with the slight breeze. The six chairs of the dining room table have been stacked seat to seat and pushed against the wall next to the china cabinet. Mar wonders if they were moved to ease the cleaning and not returned, Marta figuring that she was being paid to dust an empty house and not to maintain illusions. Or is this Marta's developed routine? On her next visit will she put back what she has moved?

The refrigerator has been unplugged and its doors opened, a pink Post-it note with medication dosages still taped to the butter door. She sticks her head in the freezer and inhales, runs her thumb over the white plastic of the top shelf.

One new message blinks on the machine but she bypasses this to walk the hallway that leads to the bedrooms. Her door is cracked and she sees the corner of her bed and the same red-flowered comforter she had used since junior high. When she opens her father's bedroom door there is a flood of light and a king bed stripped to the mattress pad. The last time she was in this space it still smelled of lilies. There had been a roomful and wanting to be alone she volunteered to stain her fingers with the anther while her mother supervised the other preparations for her father's service.

The window that shows the back patio and a view of the city is almost the size of the wall. Marta has moved a wooden stand-alone screen from the den to block half of it. Forehead to the glass, she takes in the faint reflections of her father's room, following this suggestion until it is washed out by the sun.

It is not a good day for the city, trapped in a brown haze that spreads above the tallest buildings downtown. A housefly buzzes along the base of the frame, trying one direction thinking it may have found an exit and then pawing at the glass. A glint brings her eye to the garden beyond the patio where a man reclined in a lawn chair takes a swig of a golden-colored drink. He has a sketchpad stretched across his lap and headphones, rhythmically marking the same slightly curved line. A ponytail falls over the back of the lawn chair. It has been two years since she has seen him, but it is Teddy. Further down the path, tucked away from the neighbors' sight lines, is a red and metallic-white dome tent. Teddy takes another long drink. A pair of underwear hang heavy with water from a branch of the nearest orange tree. The phone from the kitchen rings and Mar, startled, retreats behind the screen. The volume has been turned off and she can only hear the clicks of the tape while Teddy continues to sketch.

The earlier message plays first: *Derrick gave us the update. We're glad you are on your way. Thinking of you. You gave me the devil's fright. Do call. Come for breakfast? Angela will cook corn fritters. Love you.* Then the one she has just missed: *If you are checking your messages here, do give a call. Love you.*

"Hey, Gin. I couldn't get to the phone."

"So good to hear your voice, Bear. How are you?"

"Just getting in."

"Physically. I mean physically?"

"Fine."

"Come tomorrow. I want to see your face. And I have the last batch of mail. Or I'll come to you."

"I have to check Dad's car. But let's do the next day, I need to get settled. What is that? Friday?"

"Thursday. But if you need anything in the meantime, I'm the shortest drive away." Mar begins to take the groceries out of the bag and set them on the counter. "Say ten? But check the car today. I can always send Angie for you. Or we can bring the stuff over and cook. Is the gas turned on?"

Mar crosses the kitchen to the range and waits for the blue to come. "Yes. But the car will be fine."

Mar forgets the lightness of the kitchen door and Teddy swivels around at the noise.

"What was that?" her mother asks. Mar waves and signals to him with her index finger and a smile. "Just the door, Gin," turning her back to finish the conversation, taking in the neighboring enormous, Japanese-themed house. The hill that she once played on, often hiking all the way to Mulholland, has been landscaped and fenced in with two circular paths leading to the edge of the property.

While Mar continues with her back turned, Teddy closes his sketchpad and quickly walks to the orange tree and forces his underwear into the pocket of his khaki shorts. He considers collecting his other belongings but stands with his hands behind his back and waits for Mar to finish.

"Hey, listen, the gardener's here. I'll plan on Thursday in the morning." Mar nods her head at Teddy. "I'll be fine. Looking forward to breakfast. Tell Angie hello." She takes a deep breath while clutching the phone to her chest. "I apologize for that. She talks and talks and talks."

Mar cannot help but notice the growing wet ring in his pocket.

"Ms. Gillette, I'm sorry." Teddy turns to the tent and begins again with his apology.

"The place looks incredible, Teddy. Thank you." She pulls out a chair for him to sit. "Grape juice or tap water? And if that wasn't enticing enough, the juice is warm and there's no ice."

"Water is fine."

Mar returns from the house and places two small glasses and a carafe of water on the small mosaic table, the tent in full view.

"What are you working on?" handing him the glass.

"Freelancing. With an Internet graphics company. I have to finish a typeface by Friday." When there is nothing left he is forced to rest his glass on the table. "Look," thumbing his hairline.

"I wasn't looking forward to an empty house."

"I came to get some work done. I was up here last weekend and the last two days. That's all. I swear. And I have worked extra on the front yard. I don't want you to think I was taking advantage."

"How are your parents?" filling his glass.

"My mom stopped working. She's having a little trouble with diabetes. My dad still does a few plumbing jobs, but we gave up the landscaping. Except for you."

"My dad always talked about how good they were to him. And your brother?"

"Accountant."

"I remember him when he barely came up to the table."

"Not too far past it now."

"I can't get over that house. When I was last here, they were tearing down the Judge's old place and swore it wouldn't be intrusive."

"Have you seen their running track?"

"That's what that is?" looking over her shoulder. "Jesus fucking Christ."

"The celebrity tour vans stop right there," pointing underneath the eucalyptus to the mouth of the private road. "They wait ten or fifteen minutes to see if they'll be lucky enough. You see the cameras even if it's just the maid on her coffee break."

"I didn't see your car parked in the driveway."

"I parked down the hill."

"Nonsense. Bring it up."

"I need to be going. They expected me last night."

"When are you scheduled to come back?"

"I'll set the trash out now for Friday. Next Monday."

"I'll take care of the trash, but do you have any more time to work or are these freelance projects keeping you busy?"

"If they accept, but there's usually a long turnaround. After Friday, it should be quiet."

"I want a vegetable garden down there and I'll need help with the clearing. Can you give me a few hours on Saturday? Maybe Saturday and your regular Monday. Come with an empty bed. You have a pickaxe, right?"

"I do."

"Can we use your truck for a compost run?"

"I can bring a load."

"From the city, right?"

"Yes."

"I'll pay for the gas and the time, so record it."

"I just have to—I'm sorry."

"Don't be. I mean it," she says. "Anyway, bring what else you think you might need and I'll have a look in the garage."

Mar walks through the kitchen into the dining room, giving him privacy to collect his things. In the top drawer of the china cabinet she sees a pack of her father's cigarettes and the tied manila envelope resting atop their Thanksgiving china. She hears Teddy lock the gate and closes the drawer, watches him start down the hill with his backpack on and the tent neatly bagged under his arm.

A slow-jogging man approaches from the point. Further, a collection of surfers waits on the ocean. Yesterday there had been a brief rain that remains in the cakiness of the sand as the waves mime the morning traffic on the coastal highway beyond the steep rocky path. She would ditch and come to this stretch with her boyfriend in the second semester of her senior year, half a lifetime ago when she had been accepted to Brown and figured that this was why her father paid less attention.

The shirtless jogger is now a hundred yards off. She studies the sand between her feet, digs for nothing with her finger, compelled to look up only when she can hear his turbulent exhalations. Glistening slender and bald, a monitor of sorts cinched around his upper torso, he raises his hand slightly above the waistline. She moves the hair from her face and begins a smile, but he has already passed.

She tracks this jogger as he continues toward the long-abandoned pier. Suddenly turning, for a noise in the mist of the ocean, she sees a dreaded dark body swimming to the shore a short distance from her. The body stands, naked, and walks stiffly through the calf-high surf, reaches drier sand and falls, rolls on its back, chest heaving and cocked knee, the dying waves burying themselves at its feet.

The jogger, having touched the pier, is looping back toward her and toward this body. She collects her sandals and scrabbles to the highway, adjusts her rear view to look down the beach. The jogger has knelt, seems to be touching the shoulder, delaying or encouraging a rising. She turns over the engine and makes her way through Malibu toward Santa Monica.

Gin unpacks Ambrosia apples from a canvas bag as home fries simmer on the stove. "The co-op didn't open till ten," holding on to her daughter. "Something about an administrative meeting."

"I'd been thinking about heading to the beach anyway."

"When are you going to activate your cell?"

"Where's Angela?" as she helps herself to a charred bell pepper from the cast-iron pan.

"She *called*," handing Mar one of the two jars of almond butter on the counter. "One for the fritters and one for you. I couldn't forget." Mar opens the jar right there, mixes in the oil and spoons herself a bite. "And Angie's not coming until after breakfast. Something last minute. Eat without her," making air quotes, almost dropping her wooden spoon.

Mar removes the manila envelope from her bag and places it on the kitchen counter, hands her mother the bag for the extra almond butter. "Oh, it's all not fitting in that!" with a laugh. "Tea, coffee or juice?"

"Have you got jasmine?" still touching the envelope.

"What kind of ship do you think I'm running?" shooing Mar to the patio with place settings and silverware.

Mar settles next to the plant box Angela built along the length of the terrace. Her mother comes out with the tea tray. "The fritters will just be a minute," awkwardly bending to plug the electric kettle into an extension that sits behind a potted mint. "Are you eating eggs yet? I can make eggs."

"No, no." Mar starts to say more but is overcome with an urge to vomit. Covering her mouth, she excuses herself to the bathroom where she stands over the toilet. But nothing will come. The house is cluttered with books, plants and small knickknacks, sculptures, and this room is no different. She opens the medicine cabinet and sees that the Dixie cups she had imagined are not there. She must drink from the faucet.

"Pull the screen all the way shut, dear," Gin says with her back turned as Mar returns, pouring the hot water over the loose tea in the press. "You have to shove it." She looks at her watch and then to Mar. "Wait three and a half minutes and you'll get the lightest touch of mango," holding the tin out for Mar to sniff. "Everything OK?"

"Yeah."

"So, no eggs or meat?"

"Not yet."

"You must tell me when you can eat bacon again. We have a new butcher." Mar pinches a sprig of mint and fingers it, stares at her mother. "Well, you need to eat something, darling. I can't say that?" looking to her watch. "So, nothing at all with this Derrick?"

"Where does that even come from?"

"Well, if your mother can't talk about your diet, she can at least talk about your love life."

"Is that what you think?"

"He even came and met me to take me to last year's harvest. Made sure I didn't get turned around in all that desert. And when he called to let us know you were on your way down, he was so sweet about it."

"What did he tell you?"

"Nothing. Just that he worried what it had all done to you," pouring the two cups. "A writer. Handsome," she says as Mar laughs. "Why not?"

"For one, he's married."

"Angie was married before I came along. These things happen."

"Are you working?" Mar asks.

"Don't be cruel," standing unexpectedly. "But," fiddling with the screen door, "I'm reviewing a doc for the *Chronicle*. It was in Berlin and Amsterdam but hasn't generated a buzz here." She quickly enters the house and returns with the DVD. "Angie wanted me to do a favor for a friend. The Film Market comes up in November and the press will help."

"Did I take it off its track?"

"Oh no, darling. We need to replace it all together. Angie insists on doing it herself and we all know what that means. It's about a massacre in Arkansas in the twenties that was until now considered a race riot. A nice enough young man but he knows nothing about editing."

"Raw footage?"

"Mostly photos and a voice over," swatting at an insect. "They're actually interviews with a few of the survivors. The content is there. I'll show you a piece. I would give it over but that's my only."

"So, you are working."

"Other than that, helping Angie with the copy for a show she's putting together for a new gallery on Wilshire. The car obviously is working. How's the house?"

"The house."

"I miss you is all, Bear." She reaches to fill Mar's mug. "What'd you think of Marta's curtains?"

"Just a touch."

"Godawful if you want my view. She just got it in her head."

"But not a bad idea with it empty."

"I still think it was a waste for you to insist on having her keep her schedule. I would have checked in." A buzzer that sounds like a dying bird comes from the kitchen. "Are you upset? Did I upset you?"

"No."

"Before the food burns," her mother says as she stands.

"Let me help."

"You sit and relax."

When Gin returns, Mar is examining a handful of leaves drying in a clay bowl.

"You have not changed, darling. A walk around the block with you when you were a baby would take an hour. You had to touch everything. Salt?"

"No, thank you."

Her mother delivers the last of the plates and forces the screen shut. "This should be good," looking to the bowl of drying leaves. "You know she's started meditating with an Indian. That's why the whole house smells like that shit."

"It's sage, Gin."

"Well, she'll be glad to see you. I came here one afternoon and she was burning it in one of your grandmother's bowls. That's love, I guess." Gin smiles as her daughter chews. "Be honest, as good as your father's?"

"You could use more cinnamon but I like."

"Have you any ash left for the anniversary?"

"A little."

"I would love to be there with you."

"Virginia Lee!" shouts Angela when she enters to Mar and Gin huddled on the couch in front of the computer. "Did you have to show this?" An armful of silver bangles jingle as she drops the stuffed canvas totes and throws her shoes in the basket by the door. "Oh, Bear! Let me drop this in the back and come get my proper hug." She looks again at the computer screen and shakes her head. "Really, Gin? Sometimes you are truly from another planet."

"It is dreadful stuff," Gin says to Mar in mock confidentiality as she extends both arms for Mar to help her stand. "A plate's in the kitchen, sweetie pie. Join us."

"You didn't touch the baklava!"

"I was waiting." Turning to Mar, "You must. Angie is experimenting with phyllo dough. There is lavender in the layers. Let us encourage this and not the sage."

"Now taste right away. No wine? Gin, Gin, Gin! You're making her sit through niggers getting hung and no wine?" Angela selects a bottle from a shelf under the sink and pockets the opener. "Come now, let's go outside and start over."

"You two go and I'll join in. Let me clean up."

Angela disappears to the bedroom. "Gin, dear. Have you seen my pencil can?"

Mar walks to the planter at the far end of the small covered patio and crushes a chocolate mint leaf between her fingers and spreads it over the crust of the baklava, puts a little in her mouth and hand feeds the rest to Angela.

"Are you cold?" Angela asks.

"Not at all."

"Take off the sweater. Feet on the chair."

Angela sketches the outline and then spends a minute on the details of the face. She plays with the eraser before she asks Mar what she plans to do with the house.

"I'll stay."

"Gin and I were debating that. I think it will be good. You can always tag along and be my photographer?"

"I haven't shot anything in ages. I have money saved."

"It's more than the money. The show doesn't start until February and there is plenty to do. Keep it in your head."

"I want to get the house together. I'm going to plant down by where Dad always wanted a pool."

"Edibles?"

"The sun is good. I'm thinking of popping into the nursery on Sawtelle after here."

Gin is lunging at air with a green plastic racket designed to electrocute flying insects.

"Mar is staying in the house and she is planting edibles."

Her mother comes to the screen. "What will you plant?"

"Are you listening? Edibles, she's going to plant edibles."

"Down by the pool," Mar says, smiling at their banter.

"Weeds?" Gin asks. "Are there any weeds? I'm trying to picture down there."

"The gardener. The gardener's son, I mean."

"I've met him?"

"You have. Teddy. At the service but also before."

"Well," Angela says. "Good thing this Teddy. Two doors down they have an amazing succulent garden. I'm sure they wouldn't mind. Hold that position. With your hand out. I'll just come out and say it, you look thin but not as I imagined."

She hands Mar her glass of wine, allowing her to move. Gin hovers near the sliding door. "Can't you do that another time?" Angela shouts out while she draws.

"If you fixed the motor in the fountain, we wouldn't have this infestation, darling."

"Then what, darling, would you buy on QVC? Come sit with us," holding up the pad over her head. "You look like you've seen a ghost, Ginny." Angela caresses her neck. "And you're hot as a pepper."

"I'm fine," pushing Angela's hand away. "Tell her to eat, she'll listen to you," extending to kill another bug.

"Stop with that," Angela says, wresting her work from Gin. "I love the shoulder line," she says to herself. "What do you think, Mar? I'll fill in the rest."

"Can I have it like that?"

"Just the line? Let me at least spray it."

"If I want to make the nursery and miss all the traffic, I should go soonish."

"Well, when are you digging up things?"

"The fun stuff should start on Monday."

"I'll bring this and some clippings."

"Mar, *do not* let her take over," Gin says from the washroom where she is folding hand towels. "You'll have a garden of sage and ganja."

143

"There could be worse things," Angela says as she embraces Mar, digging into the muscles of her shoulders.

Two tote bags stuffed full with pre-prepared meals sit by the door. Gin walks Mar to the car, helping with a bag of the food. "I almost forgot," patting the leather of the Mercedes' door and crossing the pebbled walk for yet another tote.

"The last of the mail," hands trembling as she holds Mar's head and leans to kiss it.

"Thank you for taking care of all this."

Gin retreats to the house as Mar starts the car. The envelope she had set on the counter is among the mail her mother has collected. She fingers its caked, now half-gone cardboard clasp. When she realizes her mother remains at the door, she begins the drive to the nursery.

In the center lane of Interstate 210 toward the Lopez Canyon Landfill, Teddy, perhaps also enraptured beneath the majestically barren San Gabriels, misses the Paxton Street exit and must continue to Osborne and double back along Foothill Boulevard. He looks away from that segment of street, up and to his left, to the ridge, beyond which he can imagine the park where his father would take him and his brother as children to play a little ball the few times a year they made it out this way for compost.

At near five thirty in the morning Mar sits at the kitchen island sorting through the last of the mail. A draft from the window over the sink catches the burner's flame. She opens a credit card bill in her father's name, throws the rest in the bin as the pot starts its rattle. She lowers the flame and walks to the telephone, dials and listens while ladling herself a cup. Pieces of rosemary float to the top, one sticks to her finger and she puts it to her mouth before drinking her father, in essence, as she has these last two years.

Mar takes her tea to the mosaic patio table, the sun and remnants of morning mist on her as she reads the same secondhand tale of a refugee from the Sudan that she had started on the first day of her hunger strike nearly a month ago.

The roof of a red sedan disappears around the bend of the private road below. Mar sheds her forest-green terrycloth robe on the kitchen floor and comes to meet Angela, who is raising her chin above the wheel to help her car to the top of the driveway. Plant starts arranged in filing box tops cover the backseat.

"Bags first!"

"What's all this?"

"You sound like Gin," pinching Mar's hip. "This one is for the garden. Here, you take these two. And this is for the fridge. Is your man here?"

"Not till ten." Mar notices a wrist brace and takes the bag Angela carries in that arm. "Has time gone ahead?"

"Sunday after next."

They walk between the orange trees to the patio where she had been reading.

"I haven't been back here since you had that great big ridgeback. What a dumb cute dog he was."

Angela gasps at the neighbor's new construction as she comes down the stairs.

"Crazy, right?"

"You know they sent your father a basket when they heard about his chemo? Candied popcorn and everything else that might make you throw up. I

146

remember your father joking that they were trying to expedite it." Angela turns to look at the city. "Here, give me that," taking the bag Mar had taken from her, "and drop those inside, in the freezer. We made some pesto and a lasagna."

Mar fills the teapot and gazes out the windows that face the street until the kettle whistles her back.

Angela has opened a pastry box. "I brought the guava cheese rolls you love and even a few of the patties if you decide to eat any meat. You can freeze them."

"What's Gin up to today?"

"Final edits on that piece in the *Chronicle*. For the best, she's all nerves sometimes, just give her a sec to ease into you being back." Angela takes a patty.

"Do you miss it? The desert?"

"I thought I would."

"I couldn't be prouder of you. At some point you got to make your space."

"The world still follows," Mar says. "But your perspective does change. Everyone said it was suicide. To take that time away from the market, the lab. But people are reaching out, have been since the first harvest. I might apply for a grant, something in the city, adjunct."

"Two years next Tuesday," Angela says. "I feel foolish to say that I haven't even begun to work it through."

Mar looks to the den. "Did you come with Gin? At the end."

"Twice. I kissed your sweet father's head and sat with him. He would smile."

"She wanted to be here alone."

"He wanted to be alone. She handled that well. They worked well. I cooked."

"Does she talk much about it?"

"Only as it relates to you, her role. You know your mother," she says while Mar still looks away. "Bear, he didn't want to bother you. Sounds silly, I know. Gin argued with him, believe me she did."

"I'm not mad at her. Not about that. I don't know how to tell her that. It's on the edge of everything she says."

"If you ask me, he didn't think it was as it was. Who knows? The day my mother died she changed purses. During her life she had only the good Lord

147

knows what in these big bags. Bags would be the word. But she wanted this small thing going to the hospital and stuffed everything in it," laughing. "Who knows if she knew she was dying and wanted at last to appear proper or if she wanted a small purse to make her escape, pack light."

"I just don't know where to put everything."

"That takes a certain privacy, and she takes it personally. Your mother's a bit of a child that way, we know that. But it doesn't change her heart," wiping her hands clear of the grease from the patty. "Tell me what we've got here," standing and pointing to the left of the eucalyptus.

"We've got to clear the ivy. I'm thinking two beds, not exact, a few curved paths," pulling a napkin from her pocket that has a map.

"This circle?"

Mar points to a patch of milkweed. "I'll pull that to make room for a rosemary bed. That's what I wanted the sand for."

"Oh, but I like that."

"It'll pop up somewhere else, I promise."

"Well, I couldn't find the small bag. The man at the store nearly broke his back getting it in the car. We'll wait for help."

"Teddy."

"Yes, Teddy."

They sit halfway down the steps, Angela above with an elbow between Mar's shoulder blades, Mar picking at the threads of her jean shorts.

"How much time till we plant?"

"Evening if we're lucky. The ivy is deceptive. Then mix in the compost, Teddy is bringing a truckload. If I have to start tomorrow, so be it."

"I have acupuncture at one across town."

"You've done enough filling your car like that. I thought I'd have done more by now."

"Did you take a before picture?"

"No."

"Shame on you, Bear!" returning to the table for her camera as Teddy's red truck turns up the private road.

He wears jeans tucked into dark galoshes, a second white T-shirt in one hand and a pickaxe and shovel in the other. He hangs the shirt on a branch of an orange tree and comes down the steps.

"Now Mar swears we met but I don't remember," Angela says.

"I was small."

"I'll take your word," handing him the camera. "A picture of us," walking Mar down a few steps. "From above. Be sure to get what will be the garden in the background."

"Have you ever wondered why the digital camera reproduces the click?" Angela asks no one in particular as Teddy takes the photo.

"It's a comfort," he says as he returns the camera.

"There are some pastries. Please have some."

"I ate before I came."

"Oh, don't be polite."

"We can heat them up for lunch," Mar interjects.

"Cuban," Angela says to Teddy. "I was sure I could convince this child to eat meat. I was in Glendale, don't ask me why."

The three stand atop the stairs that descend to what her father had intended to be a pool, now overgrown with ivy, milkweed and laurel sumac weeds-turned-trees.

"So what's first?" Angela asks.

They clear Angela's car so she will be free to leave for her appointment. Teddy moves Mar's father's Adirondack chair near to where they will put the rosemary so she can sketch in the meantime. Mar attacks the ivy, clipping and untangling, and piles it against the property fence while Teddy shovels compost from the truck bed to his worn canvas tarp, cinching it and throwing each load over his shoulder to carry it to the garden.

"Did you come from Griffith?" Angela asks.

"Lopez Canyon."

"Lopez Canyon?" Mar asks.

"In Lake View Terrace. Griffith uses the manure from the zoo but adds biosolids."

"Lake View Terrace, like out near Simi Valley?" Mar asks.

"Biosolids?" Angela says to herself. "I assumed they stopped doing that," rising to bury a hand into the warm dark pile.

"I've used it for the rest of the place," pointing to the other side of the hillside where he had hidden his tent. "Lopez Canyon only adds the manure from the local stables. And we have a friend that gives us what they sell to the Westside nurseries."

"If you're going to eat it, no human shit. Seems like a good rule of thumb," Angela says.

"What time did you get up to make it all that way and back?" Mar asks.

"Yesterday. I went midday to miss traffic. My friend works during the week. Just the free pile is open on the weekends."

"Well, I'm paying you double for today. I feel bad you went so far out of your way, shit or no shit."

"Please don't. Without traffic it's not too bad."

"Mar was telling me about some design work you are doing."

"Just a proposal," Teddy says, wondering if his staying on the property has been mentioned as he talks about the digital foundry that develops for high-end art books.

"You should have him do the signage for the show," Mar says.

"That could work." Turning to Teddy, "How many have you developed?"

"That ended up in print? Seven. But loads more than that."

"Are we throwing the ivy in the green or black?" Mar asks.

"We could cover it for now, let it decompose a little and add it to a compost later."

"No, let's just throw it in the green."

"I'd love to see your work," Angela says.

They have left the sumac that have sprouted up on the north gate of the property as it will not block any of the sun but shade the garden from the overhanging deck the neighbors have built to watch the city. Mar will be forced to cut these back for the next fire season, but that is months away.

Angela and her belongings are gone from the Adirondack when they return from the waste bins. "You need to fill your ice trays, darling," walking down the steps with two cups and a pitcher of water. "But it's cold enough. And you need to drink."

Teddy hurries to take this all from her.

"Where did you find this?" Mar asks.

"The china closet. The place is immaculate."

She collects her sketchpad and walks with Mar to the car. "Oh! I almost forgot," handing Mar a pair of pruning shears from a small crumpled brown paper bag in her purse. "Japanese with a lifetime warranty, a gift from us. And make sure you document this," handing her the camera. "Bring it with the next

150

time I see you."

Mar returns to Teddy jumping in the bin to compress the vines. "You made quite the impression," giving him her hand to help him out.

"We got a bit to go. I don't think it's all going to fit. We could ask the neighbors for theirs," he says. "Or I can take it with in the truck."

"Just leave it. I'll put it in next week. At least it'll be cleared from below." Mar takes an orange from the tree, peels it and offers Teddy half. "Remember when we used to toss these on the road?"

"It would be target practice with the tour vans these days."

Teddy takes a scarred and oiled machete from his belt and hacks at the line that Mar had imagined, Mar taking what he has cut to rest between the orange trees. Soon he is pickaxing the earth, throwing the visible roots to the fence. Mar follows this with a hard rake, pushing and punching the dirt, pleased by how effortlessly the clots breaks apart. When she has made one pass, she starts again.

Teddy shovels the compost while Mar blends with the rake. When they reach the rosemary bed, he mixes a half bag of the sand. "As deep as you can," she reminds him.

She comes from the house with a check for two hundred dollars. "Not even a discussion. This would have taken days, and the compost alone."

"Still plenty of light "

"I want to start early in the day."

Teddy sprays an arc of water from above the hillside to settle the dirt, takes off his shirt and washes his chest. Shaking his hands to the wind, he walks to the orange tree.

"You don't have to do that out here," she says from the table.

"Already finished."

"I want to offer you something to drink but all I got is whiskey."

He tugs where his clean shirt has stuck to his wet skin.

"Is that a yes?"

"Do you have sugar?"

"I do."

She returns with a bottle and a mason jar with sugar. "We lucked out with the weather," she says. He has picked two oranges, halves one with a pocketknife. "So what's your vision with the typography?"

"Independent but wired to visible projects. Wouldn't want to start my own house or anything like that," arranging the glasses, squeezing the juice of half an orange into each before stirring in sugar to make a syrup.

"Are you still with your parents?"

"I live in an apartment in the building they own and manage," adding the whiskey. "They live across the street in a duplex. I do most of the work these days, since my dad's back is hit or miss."

"To you. I can't thank you enough for your help today," raising her glass. "You got to look me in the eyes, you know that. And don't be shy, eat!"

"So what are you planting?"

"Bok choy, carrots, beets, Swiss chard, cucumbers, snap peas, radish, eventually a Santa Rosa plum in that corner," pointing to a space beyond where the sumac have colonized. "And the mature rosemary."

"Now what's the deal with Angela?"

"Deal?"

"What's her work like?"

"She helps produce shows for a few galleries in Santa Monica. By the way, she meant what she said."

"She's your mom's partner, right? When did that happen?"

"Happen. I like that. I was still in elementary when I first met her. She is a sweetheart," standing to drag her lawn chair. "Let's move to the shade."

They lie on their backs in silence. Mar curls on her side and falls asleep.

After twenty minutes, he taps her finger, holds his hand there. "I hate to rush but my family is expecting me, was expecting me."

"Finish your water," rubbing her eyes.

He ties his hair and Mar grabs him by the wrist. "Come through the house," she says. "Here she is. This is a few years after they met." It is a picture of Angela and her mother when Mar was about twelve. His eyes move to another picture.

"Is this Bob?"

"My dad was part of the team that tried to bring him to the US. That's in Vegas. My mother was pregnant when this photo was taken, supposedly furious with his wanting to name me, though she disputes that."

"Funny, I never think about him when I say your name."

"It's been Mar my whole life. It was his frat boy tattoo."

152

She walks him to the door, then punctures the bottom of an empty one-gallon jug, fills it and waters the starts they had moved to the shade. Sloppy, spilling, she takes several trips, leaves her wet shoes on the steps and goes into the house.

She walks down the worn wooden steps as old as she is, crouches and sticks a finger to the wet soil. Sitting in the Adirondack, the tops of downtown buildings sprout out of the hills. It is not what she imagined. She turns the chair to instead face the overgrown hillside, picks up the shovel by the head and measures the depth of the bagged rosemary against the handle. While on the plain she had kept this shrub small, populating the surrounding desert with its trimmings. It had been repotted once but that was over a year ago and so she must rip at the roots, giving it air, before settling it into place. She collects dirt to make a wall to trap the water and sits with eyes closed as her rosemary is drip-fed, waking after more than an hour to a chill.

In the week she has been home this is the first time she has entered this room. She walks to the cubbyhole in the back where he kept his office, places the envelope and her napkin of food on the desk and turns on the birdlike lamp. It is a flat desk with no drawers. She had often thought drawers to be her father's late-blooming phobia. When she moved away for college, he rebuilt the kitchen without them, tore down a wall of cabinetry for the island. She returned to find the utensils in ceramic containers on the counters. Whatever was on this desk has been removed, perhaps in cleaning for the service.

It is not the den of her childhood. At the two large windows that open to the patio she looks down at a rectangle of the blond wood floor that is darker than the rest. The bookshelf that once sat here is no longer. Mar does not know if her mother had it moved to the garage or to the basement, or what has happened to the albums it contained. This was to accommodate her father's hospital bed. This, with the exile of the couch and love seat to the periphery, made it easier for her father to be rolled around, to follow or avoid the sun the last weeks.

When she came home for the final time her father had already been moved. Her mother told her, before she would let her in the front door, that it had become too difficult to sustain him in his bedroom. And that since hospice care had arrived, and with it the hospital bed, they had stopped the uncomfortable lifting of his body into a wheelchair so that he could enjoy the light of this room. When Mar arrived, the wheelchair had been repurposed as the seat that her mother used to read to him. For most of the day the light in the bedroom would put him to sweat, she said. The hospice nurse, whom Mar met only once, was contracted to come twice a week and seemed to second the decision. This eased the caring, they said, though she was certain her father understood the implications of his new geography.

She was never alone with him, not for any long stretch those last eleven days, except in the nights when her mother would take the monitor and sleep across the house in her father's bedroom. It was in the night that he found his words and would mutter them restlessly. Mar slept on the couch, afraid that she would be called to handle him. She just now remembers a line from that conversation before the front door was opened: *To die in one's back bedroom? No matter how many windows it had.* This, too, she supposes, was her mother's ass-backward way of softening a blow.

Mar toes a divot. She bends, picks at it and comes away with fiber, looks to the clouds that cover the city lights and sits with the nigrescent beyond. She imagines this divot was where the wheel Gin would lock struck as she pivoted the bed, talking with a strained joy to her father, to face the city.

Mar had slept in this room, in his new bed, alone in the house for five days before the medical supply truck made its way up the hill to evict her from it, clipping the branches of two trees and spilling them into the road. Only then did she return to Phoenix, to the lab, to give notice. She bought the trailer and hooked it to her truck and made her way to the plain, stopping in Los Angeles for the service her mother had arranged.

The sliding door had been opened and seats bought for both inside and outside but still people had to stand. Her father's sister had flown from Seattle and sat on the steps, the furthest away. It was the first time Mar had seen her in six years. Housekeepers she had never met served food on thick plastic plates. Marta was a guest. Teddy was there with his mother and father and brother, dressed for church. When people were invited to share, Teddy's father, whose grumbled voice was always hard for Mar to decipher, said something in an English broken by emotion as much as custom. An enormous African drum remains in the corner. She remembers an old assistant of her father with a toddler. After the informal sharing, she saw this woman lifting her child to bang on the drum as a crowd gathered. Mar wanted to tell the woman that she was raising a devil but disappeared to sit on the floor of her father's bedroom and smell the remnants of lilies.

Inside the envelope is the booklet for the funeral of Deondre Ward. Cheap, done at a copy shop. She opens the bi-fold and a receipt falls to the floor, a faded column of numbers that totals out at $464. She holds this soft twenty-year-old slip. *Best BBQ 5/8/92* handwritten in red ink by her father. There is the photo of a boy in his teens, eighteen months younger than herself then, with a green polo, caramel skin and loose curly hair, a school portrait with a gray marbled background. There is a poem followed by a list of speakers and a map for the internment, a tick mark next to a speaker's name and, next to this, more red-inked words: *brave caring loved*

Just past five she wakes on the couch, curled inside her thick terrycloth skin. She brews her tea and goes to the Adirondack. She waits until six thirty so that she can witness the coming of the morning light. The low hanging branches of the eucalyptus filter much of it. She pulls one down, in the garage finds a ladder that will reach more, but there are others, thicker, farther up. She lays the ladder on its side and sits by the rosemary.

Teddy turns into the driveway and cuts the engine. Music plays as he unhooks his ladder for the branch Mar has asked him to cut. While he works on a stubborn electric-blue cord she shuts the front door and makes the terracotta path. "Should I move closer to the trash," he shouts over the radio, thinking that he had not left room enough.

Wearing a shoulder purse and carrying a grocery bag she sets an elbow on the hot metal of the truck bed. "How long do I have you for?"

"The afternoon."

"I want your help for an errand. Then I take you to lunch and we come back to cut the tree. Yes?"

"My car?"

"But I pay for gas and food. You can leave the ladder against the garage."

"Freeway or streets?" he asks as they are heading down the private road.

"We want to end up on the 110 South." She looks in her purse and opens a small notebook. "We get off at Long Beach Ave."

"I didn't wake up today thinking I was going to Compton."

She laughs, looks out the window as the suspension bounces the truck down the hill.

They settle in the middle lane, beginning to pass downtown when Mar comes out with it: "I think my dad had another kid who is buried down there. We're going to a cemetery."

"Fuck," he blurts. "I mean, it's alright."

"I know it seems crazy asking you to come with."

After a moment, "My dad didn't marry my mom until he was in his late forties. Sometimes I wonder."

"My dad respected your father so much. They talked a lot, you know. Out there in the yard. The two of them smoking. Has he quit?"

"That's what he tells my mom. But he comes into my room."

"This one would have been my age."

"How long ago since you lived here?"

"I left right after I finished grad school and went to Phoenix. Seven and a half. But that was just for a year when I was applying. So it's been since high school, really. More than fifteen years. Before all this was here anyway," pointing to the downtown growth. "You have any thoughts of moving?"

"My parents are getting older. I have a girlfriend, even though we are going through it right now."

"What does she do?"

"Works at the same bank as my brother. Citi. Different branch now, but that's how we met."

"Serious?"

"I don't know. You?"

"Relationship? No. I had a pretty serious one back in Phoenix but when I left, I just left. He didn't even know my dad was sick. I quit and skipped town without even telling him anything. Sent an email a few weeks later. I should've felt ashamed but I didn't. Don't." She examines her printed directions. "What about you? The most shameful thing you've done?"

"I'm sure I have done a lot, but I never left a boy high and dry in Phoenix."

"Never got caught stealing a pack of gum?"

"No." From the freeway Teddy can see the clinic that he and Rosie visited yesterday and will return to Friday. "Was it Long Beach?"

"Yeah, and we want to go left off the freeway. We're looking for Abby Memorial. It says it's about a mile on the right."

"It's still a bit. My parent's first apartment was in Wilmington, the next town over. My Mom was pregnant with me. And the town my family came from is small, farms. In the eighties this was the heart of the violence. They got out before I turned one."

There is a booth at the entrance, a guard stationed in front of a rusted desk fan. He collects his clipboard and comes to the window of the truck. Teddy points to Mar. "We are here to look at a grave," she says.

"Month and year."

"Excuse me?"

"Death date."

"April 1992."

He unhooks the pen from his clipboard and asks her for the deceased's full name, returns to the small guardhouse where he puts on reading glasses and leans to a small screen and pecks at a keyboard. He motions for Teddy to back up and takes down his plate, hands them a sheet with the number of a grave.

"A map is on the back but you won't need it. Take that road and park right after the bend. The row numbers are painted on the sidewalk. Look for this number. And forty-nine is about a third of the way." Teddy thanks him as he accepts the paper. "We close at five today."

"We won't be long, sir," Mar says.

She takes her purse and walks to the plot as Teddy keeps watch from the car. She picks up a half-buried plastic flowerpot with a long-withered plant. She yanks bunches of the dry grass that obscure the face of the stone, stands and looks down at it. The cemetery is on a slight hill that shows the way they came, but the smog hides the mountains. On the walk back the remains of the potted plant swing in her right hand.

"Are you hungry?"

"I could eat," Teddy says.

"But stop at the gate."

She crosses in front of the truck to the guardhouse where the man comes out to meet her. She asks him about the upkeep. He apologizes for the conditions, explains that they have been splitting a crew between two properties. "And then came the heat," he adds as she shades the low sun with the manila envelope she has carried with her. "They're due day after next, but I can't be certain when they will get to each plot. It should be once a month, but with the overload and the short staff. There's a man who brings flowers and keeps the site clean and takes pictures for the Internet. Do you want his card?"

"That'd be nice."

He walks around the guardhouse to search the desk, taking off his hat and rubbing his brow with the sleeve of his uniform. "Here you go, ma'am." His lips purse as if he is about to speak more.

"Sir, do you know of a Best BBQ near here?" she asks. "I couldn't find an address."

"That's because they changed the name. The son took it over a few years back. Just as good though. Right out of here. Two streets and another right," motioning with his hands. "Left side."

"Thank you."

"Can't miss it. Halfway down the block, you'll see the smokers in the parking lot."

She waves another thanks and starts for the truck when she thinks she has

160

heard him. She turns, the envelope still shading her face.

"Do you mind me asking how you knew Mr. Ward?"

"A relation of my father," as if she had prepared for the question.

"He was one of the boys killed by the police in the rebellion?"

"I hadn't thought," swallowing the words as she speaks them.

"I'm sorry, miss, not my place. That's not my place."

He turns toward the guardhouse. She stands for a moment and then makes her way back to the truck where she concentrates on the business card, flipping it over before placing it in her envelope. "It's a right out of the driveway," she says.

"I thought you didn't eat meat."

"I haven't in about two years. But this place is good. Not so saucy, at least from what I remember."

"You've been here?"

"As a teenager this was always a treat. We never came here but he would always bring it to the house, maybe three times a year. I thought one of his studios was down here. Maybe there was."

The walls are adorned with pictures of the local football team. They look at the menu painted above the glass enclosure and decide to split the tri-tip combo and a cobbler. They sit outside, on the covered patio with three wooden picnic benches and another couple.

"You're sure?" looking in the direction of the cemetery.

"He left things for me."

"I got one if you still want to hear it."

"One what?"

"A shame."

"Yes, please," she says with soft wrinkles showing at the corner of her eyes.

"Thanksgiving break of sophomore year. My parents thought I was home studying for exams. Me and my buddies got cheap tickets to Cancún because of the hurricane season."

"Sounds promising," Mar laughs.

"Well, we were out of danger, but a big one had hit and the hotel zone was still recovering so we got rooms for nothing. Three days of drinking and the beach. The second night we were on the road where the taxis go from hotel

161

to hotel outside the gates. It's where the local kids come begging for money. There were a ton of kids. Brian was my roommate, the one who paid for almost my whole trip. He was shirtless and drunk, and he starts chasing this little frog. After the rain, they're all in the streets. He was muttering about *local pussy*. He kept at this all weekend, local pussy. Stupid fucking kids. Anyway, he can't catch the frog. Partly because he's drunk off his ass, but mostly because they jump and they're small and it's dark."

"You can talk and eat. I won't think less of you."

"One of these kids comes and scoops it up, the frog, and gives it to Brian. Have you ever touched a frog?"

"Hasn't everybody?"

"Well, as soon as Brian touches the thing he throws it and starts jumping around. The kid follows him with his hand out. I say he wants money, laughing but feeling sorry for the kid. Another one of our friends. I can see his face. Thick-rimmed glasses, red hair. Always smoked pot. He gets the idea to find a stick and have these kids round up a bucketful of frogs and we play baseball. Only he's drunk, grabbing this kid, mimicking swinging a bat and no one can figure out what the fuck is going on. The red head's girlfriend came down. The only girl on the trip. I remember Brian was furious at that. Anyway, I had to translate and negotiate with these kids. One ran to get a bucket and started collecting. Only thing was, no one wanted to touch the frogs. None of us. So we paid a kid to pitch frogs. We got big rocks from off the road and lined up bases. We didn't even have sides. It was just a bunch of drunk kids swinging at frogs."

"Did you hit them?"

"Does it really matter?"

"To the frog, I imagine"

"They were hard to hit because all we had was a tree branch, about this thick, and, like I said, it was pitch black," staring beyond Mar's shoulder. "But I did hit one. Not flush, I didn't even look where it went or what happened to it. They would all be quiet and wait for the sound. Brian, before each person got up, would flap his arms like he was a quarterback. You know, hushing everyone. Then he would tap the little kid throwing the frogs. After the sound, the red head would just start yelling *power stroke, power stroke!* His girlfriend just sat off by herself against the wall of the hotel. I remember the look on her face when I stopped at the first rock, out of breath after a full sprint and with acid in my throat. I thought about my parents. The security came and said it wasn't safe for us to be beyond the wall and we went inside to the pool and Brian couldn't stop laughing. I've done a lot of stupid regrettable shit," he says. "But that's what comes back, the look on the girl's face."

The drive home is with traffic and they don't reach until after five. The car idles in the driveway. "Thank you for doing that with me." She grabs his wrist and turns to give him a hug. "The tree another day," she says. "What's your time tomorrow?"

"The morning. I'm free in the morning."

"Or next week, the regular time."

"Tomorrow is fine."

She looks in the bed. "You can pitch your tent," she says. "Seriously, there's an extra bedroom. Do it first thing," starting to open the door. "Look, I don't want to cause problems but you are welcome."

He collects his hair in a ponytail, ties it with the leather band.

"The least I can do is pour you a drink," she says. "No food but we can order."

Seven in the morning and Mar is in the kitchen searching for towing companies in San Luis Obispo. Only two chairs are at the table, the other four stacked where Marta, whom she had thanked and mailed a check and given the month off, left them. The curtains have been folded and boxed for when she returns. In the pantry are glass jars with the grains that would make up her father's morning porridge. They are labeled in her mother's writing on masking tape in thick green marker. A Post-it with measurements is stuck on the lid of the amaranth.

She covers the simmering pot and takes the phone and her notes outside. She is reading off the VIN as Teddy appears at the kitchen steps wearing only his jeans.

"Do you wanna go for a walk?"

"I have something on the stove," with a hand over the phone. "You go and I'll finish up here and we will breakfast when you get back?"

He pauses at the hall mirror, sets his hair behind his shoulders, and walks down past the house where he and Mar used to aim their oranges. There is an overgrowth of chamomile near to the concrete wall. He breaks off a stem to spin in his hand and continues his walk. The neighboring property has been razed, the foundation of some new enormous thing dug. A dumpster with bits of wood and cinder block waiting to be collected is all that remains. He sits on the property's railed edge looking at people walking along the ridge of the next canyon as he scrolls through the messages on his phone.

On his way back, after the first bend in the private road, he hears an engine make the turn and takes his stride to the side. A private security car comes along side. "Do you live here?" from an opening window. There is no malice in the man's tone, but Teddy is nonetheless deliberately silent. "There has been a complaint."

"Visiting a friend," pointing up the road.

The officer follows Teddy to the driveway where Mar has already come to the terracotta path.

"What's the problem?"

"Miss, a resident complained and we are obligated to follow up. There's no issue. With the construction there's been some insecurity."

"Which resident?"

"I can't divulge that."

"Bullshit," as he starts to speak of company policy. "What was the complaint?"

"That there was a man loitering in front of their property. Cutting plants."

"Is this a fucking joke?"

"There are no problems here, miss."

The neighbor's garage opens as they are leaving for the morning and Teddy walks inside.

"Inside or outside?" she asks while mashing blueberries for their breakfast.

"Inside is fine."

"Can you fucking believe it?"

"Do you need help?"

"I'm just waiting for the walnuts to finish. The fucking nerve." She opens the oven to grind salt on the tray. "Yogurt?"

"What do you put on?"

She prepares her bowl.

"About half that," he says before they bury what little words they have in the porridge.

He breaks the silence with talk of tree branches. She insists that they can do this another day. "Don't be ridiculous," he says.

"When do you have to get back?"

"In a bit. There's a leak in a unit but my dad turned off the water."

"We can do the tree later."

"I'll take it down and come next Monday with the chainsaw," he says. She crumbles a few more walnuts in her hand and splits the pieces between them. "This tastes a lot better than it looks," he says. "C'mon," standing and taking the bowls to the sink.

"I'll wash later," she says.

He rinses his hands, drying them on his jeans before he ties his hair and returns to the truck for his saw.

By ten the traffic is thin. Mar parks just north of the enclave of Hasidic Jews and television producers, walks the half block to where her mother is waiting at a street-side table with a carafe of orange juice. She comes into the sidewalk, draped in a lavender shawl, her arms raised like a tottering crow. Even before they embrace she is talking nervously about the light fog. "You're looking fuller," adjusting the chair on the slanted concrete.

Mar sets her sunglasses on the table and spreads the cloth napkin over her thighs.

"So, the garden?" Gin offers. "Angie says it's going to look spectacular."

Mar picks a hair that must be Teddy's from the cuff of her white button-down, turns it over between her fingers until it is a loose black ball and lets it fall to the sidewalk.

"It appears you've been eating. That's all I wanted to say. I can't ask that?"

"You can."

"To you being home."

Mar raises the glass to her lips and asks if Angela is in the gallery.

"May have slept there," Gin says.

"She asked me to shoot for her. Does she need the help or is she trying to keep me busy?"

"Probably a little of both, but darling I can handle the shooting. Put something in my hands, you know. You just come."

"It's good."

"Come now?"

"The juice."

"Thank you for coming down."

"I wasn't doing much of anything and I'm due for a shop."

"I'm worried you are cooped up on the hill. Angie says it too. I'm just glad to see you."

Mar picks up the oversized menu lying across her plate. "You have to trust that I'm fine."

"So you turned the Internet back on?"

"Never turned off."

"But I've sent you every piece of mail."

"It's a bit of a clusterfuck but not your fault. He paid a year at a time."

Gin holds the carafe in the air to signal to the waiter who is cleaning an inside table near to the window.

"That's your father. I bet it saved him five dollars."

"It came due last month. Some obscure card I'd never seen. It was in the last stack you gave me. I tried to close the account but they had me on hold for so long I just put a check in the mail."

"Figure your food," Gin says while searching her agenda.

"Did you finish the piece on the documentary?"

"God yes," her eyes straying to a St. Bernard pissing on the palm a few feet from their table. "I'll send you the proof. They picked an image that doesn't quite match but my good deed is done."

Mar reaches across the table to tuck a strand of her mother's hair behind her ear. "When did you go?"

"You like it?"

"The color is great."

"I had Leslie leave a little more of the gray."

The owner comes to the table. "Eduard, this is my daughter," Gin says as he rubs the back of her shoulders. "She is overwhelmed."

"We love your mother. Breakfast or lunch?"

"I've asked."

"Two minutes," Mar says. He walks away, talks to the cashier who brings a complimentary almond croissant.

"I'm fine with just this," Mar says to her mother.

"Order something, dear. It's the polite thing."

Gin hands Mar a photo. It is of Mar's parents sitting outside a different restaurant. "Angie developed a roll last week. We thought it was for the show."

Mar stares out into the traffic and rubs a crease in the corner of the photo with her thumb, a heat rising in her neck.

"What am I supposed to do with this?"

A hand is on her shoulder, Eduard asking if she has decided. Setting the photo beside the half-eaten croissant, "The quiche, is it big?"

"As big as you like."

She closes the menu and hands it to him. "A small piece, thank you."

"Citrus or oil and vinegar?"

"Just the quiche if I can."

"You can give me the salad," Gin says. "Citrus. Thank you, Eduard."

Gin reaches to take back the photo. "The final day of the chemo. Late July. The 27th. I had to figure it this morning. It was a Friday. He had all the nurses swooning. We just knew you would be home for Thanksgiving and everything would have been laid out." She strokes the bridge of her nose. "We just knew."

Mar can only look to the street.

"We are at the cheese shop off Rowena," her mother continues. "He insisted on taking me out for lunch and a drink even though he could only stomach a few sips. He ordered a wine they said was from Chile. And your father, you can guess the rest, he had them bring out the bottle. The poor kid was so embarrassed. He made him sit and have a glass with us."

Another waiter, boyish, interrupts with Mar's food and a new carafe. "They squeeze it on the hour, darling. Have some more."

"I don't want any fucking orange juice," escaping to the bathroom.

Gin busies herself, puts the picture and her agenda away in her purse, unfolds a napkin and covers Mar's quiche, looks through the glass to the bathroom.

"Why do you think I would want this?" speaking before she has even pulled her chair in.

"Angie says—"

"Seriously?" She starts with her quiche but is compelled. "Who was Deondre, Mom?"

"What on earth are you talking about, darling?"

"Dad would choke on his name over and over."

"I honestly don't recall."

The boy brings the benedict and Gin mutters her gratitude.

"Was it the same before I came?"

"What?"

"The talking, Mom."

Gin moves the salad around with her fork. "Yes."

"That's all he said those days I was there. At the end in his sleep. If he was sleeping."

168

"I'm sorry I've offended you, but that was the aphasia, darling. One word would stand for a thousand."

"I know what it is."

"I learned to hear it as noise. It still eats me that they never scanned the brain. Let me buy you something for the garden."

"I don't need anything for the garden."

"I hear you are transplanting a rosemary from the plain. They have such great ceramics."

"I put it in the ground."

"Look at that set of plates." Gin reaches across the table, kneads the tendons in her daughter's hand. "I was thinking I would come to you next week."

After a scattered walk through Ralphs, Mar is driving the hill with only a miniature organic watermelon between her legs and twenty-four rolls of toilet tissue on the passenger seat. In her rearview is the figure of a woman in the window of the walled house at the bottom of the private road, the property Mar had always called The Mansion. It is no bigger than any of the surrounding properties, especially now, but it was that it was the first to erect a wall and she was seven. She holds the clutch and falls back into the main road.

The entrance, embedded in the concrete of its wall, is a solid slab of rustic mahogany with no handle. There is a buzzer with no speaker. Not even the satisfaction of the faintest register, only a blue light from a small circle of glass above the button. She intuits that she is being watched and looks into the blue. A door opens and the sound of keys comes from the other side.

"I am here to see the owner of the house," raising to her toes as if this will help the sound carry. "A friend of mine was walking by this house yesterday. Apparently, somebody here accused him of stealing flowers and called security."

"He's not taking visitors today."

"Mr. Heir?" remembering a name that she had not thought of in over twenty years. Mar looks to the sun. "I am not sure who you are, but I have lived in this neighborhood for forty years," she says. "He called security on a houseguest of mine and I would like to address this with him."

She hears the sound of a rubber band snapping against the gloss of a magazine and only then does the mail slot in the wall become visible. "As you said, this man was stealing Mr. Heir's flowers."

Perhaps this woman has come for the mail and has no intention of addressing her. Mar speaks to the slot. "These flowers are overgrown and are on city property. If Mr. Heir prefers, I can file a report with the police."

That brings the crack of the door and the sight of the woman in jeans and a tight pink shirt with blonde curly hair tied in a messy bun.

"He's sleeping."

"When do you expect him up?"

"Sleep is not certain."

"I'll leave a note."

170

The air is cool inside the entrance hall. The woman takes off her shoes, roots Mar to this station with a whisper and enters a kitchen bathed in light where a chair has been dragged to the window. Mar hears the opening and quick shutting of a drawer, the opening of another. The woman returns with paper and pen and sets it on the half-moon oak table in the entryway, removes a phone from her bra and sends a text as Mar, her bluff called, contemplates the blank sheet. A moan followed by a string of coughs calls the woman to take a cube of gum from her pocket and retreat to the hallway. Mar takes a half step in this direction, but the woman is already behind one of the doors. She wanders into the kitchen where there are flakes of ashes tucked in the corner of the window. She taps her fingers on the stick of tobacco coating the lime green frame. Shaded by a palm tree, this window looks directly up toward the crown of the hill and her father's house. If she were to stand on the garden's steps this woman could see her clearly, perhaps has seen her clearly. There is a once-cutting-edge wood-paneled TV monitor on the counter that shows a view of the front door and the street beyond.

"That's my house. I've never seen it from here," she says as the woman appears.

There is a photo of Mr. Heir and his wife and two kids above the telephone. The woman reaches out her hand for the note. "I haven't finished," Mar says. "Are you family?"

"The nurse," unstrapping her wrist brace to announce this. Mar looks to her flip-flops with a desire to make amends, is taken aback when it is the woman who offers a cup of tea.

"I'm sorry to interrupt. I was coming from down the hill and, well, this now all feels awkward."

"The kettle goes on either way."

"How long have you been working here?" extending her hand. "Mar."

"Susan. A year."

"I just moved back."

"I took care of Mr. Heir's son's mother-in-law in England."

"So you're English?"

"South African. I used to work for a service half the year, different assignments. I got on well with her and they sent me here."

"Do you have help?"

"A man comes once a day to take him to the bathroom. But, like today,

171

he's usually late and I do it anyway. A girl on Sunday."

Mar looks at the family photo. "How is he?"

"What's that?"

"His temperament?"

The nurse returns a confused look.

"He was the neighborhood monster. You know, the one kids make up stories about. Their basements."

"I don't see kids here."

"They stay inside nowadays, I imagine. We would throw shit over his wall," laughing at her confession. "In bags. Doesn't even make sense. One time he pinned a note to our gate threatening to kill my dog. My father brought me down to confront him, thinking we were on the righteous side and he was teaching me a lesson about standing up. Mr. Heir denied it and just looked dead at me the whole time. These same eyes," turning to Susan. "Does his family come?"

"His children live in New York, a daughter in Germany. No."

Mar sees a box of hollyhocks beyond the window. "Do you plant this?"

"Oh, no. It is lovely though."

Mar leaves the car, walks the hill with the watermelon and one roll of the twenty-four, stretches in the driveway before she calls Teddy. "This is Mar," she says to his voicemail. "I'm back from our neighbor. Turns out the nurse called the cops on you. I gave her a strict talking to. Well, that's not true, but she was repentant. Anyway, I'm sorry again for yesterday. Well, not the whole. It was great having you here. But I seemed to have vomited my stuff all over you. Call when you get some time."

Teddy está sentado en la mesa del comedor con su papá mientras su mamá pela dos melones en la cocina cuando suena el timbre. La señora, limpiando un cuchillo en su mandil, va hacia la puerta. Rosie la besa, Teddy la abraza, y el señor se pone de pie, agarrando su servilleta de tela. -Come mija, dice él en su voz ronca, casi ininteligible. -Quédate. Come algo.

-Sólo un jugo -dice Teddy por ella. -Te dije, tenemos que irnos.

Rosie besa al señor y le ayuda a acomodarse en su silla, anda a la cocina para ayudar a la señora. Le da un tazón lleno de naranjas, recién lavadas y cortadas a la mitad. Empieza a exprimir el jugo, poniendo todo su peso en el extractor. Tira las cáscaras en el mismo tazón hasta que la señora empuja con su pie el bote que está usando para el melón.

-¿Cómo está tu mamá? -pregunta la señora.

-Bien, gracias. Le pasa sus saludos, tuvo que correr al trabajo.

-Fue rápida la recuperación entonces.

-Sí, al final no fue tan serio como pensamos. Gracias a Dios.

-Sí.

Ya tiene el jugo de doce naranjas. Golpea al extractor para sacar todo lo posible, echando el bagazo en el bote. La señora le pasa la jarra y la llena.

Rosie recoge los vasos, platos y tenedores -¿Para cuántos? -pregunta a la señora.

-Cuatro. David todavía está enfermo.

Los hombres suben los codos para dejar a Rosie poner la mesa. Regresa a la cocina para traer la jarra y un popote para el señor.

-Traigo lo demás -dice la señora, mandando a Rosie a sentarse a la mesa.

Teddy y su papá hablan sobre algo que paso ayer en uno de los departamentos. Rosie se posa al lado de Teddy, empieza a tocar inconscientemente el mantel. -Todo está resuelto. No pasó nada -dice Teddy a su papá.

La señora saca los bolillos del horno, los trae a la mesa.

-Quejaron como si fuera agua en todas partes -dice el señor.

-El hilo se rompió y por eso no pudo bajar.

-¿No sabía como repararlo? -pregunta la señora.

-¿Un profesor y no sabe eso? -agrega el señor.

-No ha terminado su doctorado.

Los tres se ríen. David entra y da su papá un golpe cariñoso en el hombro y un golpecito en la oreja de su hermano mayor. Teddy le pega en el pecho y David empieza a toser.

-¿Qué demonios haces tú aquí? -pregunta la mamá trayendo una mermelada de duraznos casera y el plato de melón.

-No pasa nada -dice el señor.

La señora palpa la nuca de David, dándole un masaje. -Vete a tu cuarto.

-Voy, voy -saludando a Rosie con la mano.

La señora llena su vaso de jugo, coloca unos tres pedazos de mélon sobre un plato y deseparece en el pasillo atrás de su niño.

De vuelta a la cocina, la señora pone su asiento a la esquina de la mesa acercandose al señor, tocando ligeramente su muslo. Teddy da una mordida al pan con mermelada.

-No lleva tanta azucar, pero rico, eh?

Los padres de Teddy ya no comen pan ni mermelada.

-¿Y a dónde van? -pregunta la señora.

-A la playa, mamá, te dije -dando una respuesta antes que Rosie puede decir algo.

-Es que no parecen vestidos para eso.

Ella mira a Rosie en sus jeans y su blusa de un morado obscuro.

-Ay, ma, sólo a caminar y comer. Por eso no comemos mucho.

Rosie se obsesiona con una mancha de naranja en el mantel, frotando con su servilleta mientras Teddy habla con sus padres sobre una playa imaginaria.

La señora se levanta. Regresa de la cocina con un vaso de agua mineral. -Gracias mija, dándolo a Rosie.

Rosie pone agua en la tela y empieza otra vez sus toques. No se ve ninguna mancha. Y Rosie se pregunta si había una.

-¿No vas a comer nada? -la señora pregunta a Rosie.

-Estoy bien con el jugo- poniendo la mano encima de la de Teddy -Vamos a comer muy rico en la playa.

Teddy se pone de pie bruscamente, todavía con la mitad de un bolillo en la mano.

-Pero no comiste nada de fruta -dice la señora.

-Tenemos que reunirnos con Gabo, ya.

Besa a su papá y despues a su mamá, Rosie le sigue en cada gesto.

La señora retira la fruta de la mesa y va a la cocina. Están en la puerta cuando ella regresa con una bolsa de papel doblada. La señora camina hasta la acera, mirando a su hijo abriendo la puerta de la camioneta para Rosie.

Teddy puts the bag from his mother on the seat between them and connects his phone to the stereo, hands it to Rosie to choose the music before they head north on Broadway to Planned Parenthood for the procedure.

"I had to say something. What was I going to say?"

"You could've told me."

"It just came to me."

"The beach? Did you even look at what I'm wearing?"

He puts the bag of food in the back of the cab and touches her leg.

As they follow the curve after King Boulevard, downtown appears and an incoming call rings through the speakers. He checks the phone number and sends it to voicemail. This has made him swerve into the next lane. At the stoplight the driver of a black sedan leans on his horn and hollers at them with a red face through a closed window.

Teddy raises his hand in apology but this gesture is read as indifference, or he is looking for a fight. The window comes down. "Cunt!"

Teddy yanks his door open but the light turns green and the car pulls away. "Not now," Rosie says, as Teddy speeds to catch up. It is a young kid. Rosie moves the sunshade to block anything she can of the view. At the next light Teddy glares at him, flips him off and accelerates. The kid pulls alongside again. Rosie turns up the volume to drown out his yelling just as Teddy jerks his car to scare him. The kid throws his soda at the truck and speeds off.

"It's not your fault, just not now."

"What a fucking prick."

"Just let it go."

The car is twenty yards ahead in the other lane. Teddy keeps his distance, hoping to catch a light that will separate them, but the kid swerves into his lane and slams on the brakes. Teddy pulls to the right to avoid him, but spots a man stepping off the curb wearing neon-green headphones.

He wakes to the smell of latex and the taste of rusted metal.

"Keep your head down, son."

The front of his truck is split by a lamppost. His window has been broken in the crash or by the police officer holding his mouth open with a deep purple gauze bandage.

The radio is buzzing, covered in his mother's peach jam. He reaches to shut it off but the officer applies just enough pressure for him to know that this will not be possible. The officer's latexed hand does allow him to turn his head to the right where Rosie's airbag is limp, her seat empty and its belts cut. She has been pulled to the sidewalk, her back to the concrete wall of a small neighborhood women's gym. Another cop attends to her as a Zumba class looks on through the windows. There is the pedestrian whom Teddy swerved to avoid standing next to Rosie, talking to another officer. Teddy can hear him attempt to describe the black car. Teddy wants to name the make of the car, but his mouth is full of blood and fingers that are not his own.

"Keep your head down."

More officers have appeared. One has his knee on Rosie's seat and is leaning in. "Can you move your feet?" this one asks.

"Is she OK?" before anything else can be shoved into his wound.

"Your girlfriend? She may have broken her foot, maybe a nose. But considering, she looks to be doing fine. They'll need to take her to the hospital to check for internal bleeding. Fire's on its way and we'll get you out. We don't want to move you anymore than we have to. She says a man cut you off and drove away?"

"Audi," Teddy finally says, taking the gauze from his own mouth as the guttural horn of a fire truck cuts through the distance.

On the plain her trailer gave the impression of a delicate impermanent thing. Here, perched since yesterday at the end of her driveway, it is a tumorous mass of cream-colored corrugated metal completely obstructing the view from her childhood bedroom. She only marks her mother's arrival by the shadow crossing the shuttered window.

They hug at the doorstep. Gin refuses to let her carry any of the bags at her feet. She wants to offer the surprise. "Now don't go saying anything. This is eggplant parm. And this is another baklava. This time with the mint. A bag of apples, microwaveable organic burritos but you can oven them."

"You didn't have to do all this."

"Wasn't a fuss. I was doing our shop for the week." Gin plops down at the dining room table. "I brought a witbier your father had come to like. I figured we could toast."

"The snails will be happy," Mar says. Gin does not understand. "It's for the garden, Mom. But thank you, we will toast." Mar puts all but one bottle in the fridge. "Can I get you something else to drink? I've got water. Green tea? I can squeeze some orange juice."

"I'll take some oranges with me but water for now." She pulls a stainless bottle from her purse. "Can you fill this up? The ridiculous doctor says I need to drink six of these a day. Imagine that?" Mar fills the bottle and alights on a stool around the island. "How are you, doll? Come sit near."

"A day like the rest."

"Let's eat in the garden," her mother says, smoothing the tablecloth.

Gin sits on the Adirondack, Mar on a towel she has brought for the ground. Mar pours the beer into three saucers and places them throughout the beds, explaining to Gin that she thinks she may have a snail problem by the look of a few of the young leaves. They split the rest of the warm beer as they eat toasted bagels with cream cheese and sun-dried tomatoes. Gin asks when the tree branch fell.

"It ripped as Teddy was cutting. He'll come to make it clean."

"Shame the fence got twisted like that."

"At least now the beds will have the morning light."

"What are you going to do with it? The wood?"

"I'll use some to line the rosemary. Do you want some for the fireplace?"

"Eucalyptus is divine. But only if you don't have another plan."

"There will be plenty. But you have to wait another week, he needed the week off to help his parents out."

A van pulls up to Mr. Heir's house and Mar watches the nurse hustle to meet the oversized man unloading plastic bags of medical supplies. As he enters, the nurse heads toward the property wall where Mar can only see her cigarette smoke rising. The man is there no more than ten minutes. The nurse has this timed out and walks to the front door just as he is leaving.

Gin and Mar are on the couch that remains at the den's perimeter, the peel of an orange in pieces on the couch's wooden armrest. "You know, I didn't read to him once in the eleven days," Mar says. "You read to him every morning. I couldn't stand that look in his eye," excusing herself to go to the bathroom. Gin collects the orange peels, stuffs them into her near-empty beer bottle.

Mar is on her knees in the garden. The sun, as of yesterday, an hour early and there are no dead snails in the saucers of beer, though she has finally seen the pale-yellow cabbage butterfly. Searching the half-eaten mustards and turnips, she looks for the caterpillars and their eggs as if she were inspecting a child for lice. Extracts the first, hiding along the stem of the most mature start. Studying its curl on her finger for a breath, perhaps peering its translucence to judge it female, before she presses. Leaf by leaf plant by plant until her fingertips are dirty with the mess.

A car has downshifted to work its way up the private road. She raises on her knees, wipes the compost-stained sweat from her temple with the knuckle of her thumb. An unfamiliar green truck appears at the bend, passes beneath, packed full of gardening equipment and honking as it approaches the second turn. She may have seen the leather band he keeps on his wrist. In any case, she has seen enough to trot the steps to the kitchen door without exhale, to wash the stick from her hands at the utility sink.

From the now curtainless windows of the dining room all but the tailgate of this truck has been made invisible by her quarantined trailer. The engine idles quiet. Or it has been shut off. Teddy appears, lowers the gate and with what looks like incredible effort strides into the bed and out of view. He returns, sets the blower on the gate and sits beside with feet dangling. Taking the band, he pulls his hair back and secures it, slides off the gate and shoves the blower over his shoulder. With a slight limp, perhaps from the weight of the machine, he disappears behind the trailer to the terracotta path and begins with the pine needles.

in memory of

Shirley Tanner Wilson

(1941 – 2010)

Notes

Writing from this collection was previously published in *3AM Magazine, Callaloo, The Common, Crazyhorse,* and *Stirring.*

Page 74: The "idea of ancestry" comes from Etheridge Knight's poem of the same name. "I know her dark eyes. They are mine" are lines from the poem with minor changes. "No one ever really knows his own begetting" is a variation of a line from Telemachus in Homer's *The Odyssey.*

Page 104: Hattie Carthan was a Brooklyn-based environmentalist and community activist.

Page 107: The "end of safety" comes from James Baldwin's essay "Faulkner and Desegregation."

Page 110: Charlie Haden rests against the wall.

Page 111: Sara D. Roosevelt Park encompasses a then-forgotten African American burial ground from the 18th and 19th centuries.

Page 113: Raphael's words for Lucie in the silo come in part from an interview with Arthur Jafa. "Arthur Jafa in Bloom." New York Times, April 14, 2019.

Page 145: Teddy unknowingly follows the route of Rodney King on March 3, 1991.